faith, hope,
and ivy june

Phyllis Reynolds Naylor

faith, hope, and ivy june

A YEARLING BOOK

This is a work of fiction. Names, characters, places, and incidents either are the product of the author's imagination or are used fictitiously. Any resemblance to actual persons, living or dead, events, or locales is entirely coincidental.

Text copyright © 2009 by Phyllis Reynolds Naylor
Cover art copyright © 2009 by Ericka O'Rourke

All rights reserved. Published in the United States by Yearling, an imprint of Random House Children's Books, a division of Random House, Inc., New York. Originally published in hardcover in the United States by Delacorte Press, an imprint of Random House Children's Books, New York, in 2009.

Yearling and the jumping horse design are registered trademarks of Random House, Inc.

Visit us on the Web! www.randomhouse.com/kids

Educators and librarians, for a variety of teaching tools, visit us at www.randomhouse.com/teachers

The Library of Congress has cataloged the hardcover edition of this work as follows:
Naylor, Phyllis Reynolds.
Faith, hope, and Ivy June / Phyllis Reynolds Naylor. — 1st ed.
p. cm.
Summary: During a student exchange program, seventh-graders Ivy June and Catherine share their lives, homes, and communities, and find that although their lifestyles are total opposites, they have a lot in common.
ISBN 978-0-385-73615-2 (hardcover) — ISBN 978-0-385-90588-6 (lib. bdg.) —
ISBN 978-0-375-89101-4 (ebook)
[1. Student exchange programs—Fiction. 2. Friendship—Fiction. 3. Toleration—Fiction.]
I. Title.
PZ7.N24Fai 2009
[Fic]—dc22
2008019625

ISBN 978-0-375-84491-1 (pbk.)

Printed in the United States of America
10 9 8 7 6 5 4 3 2 1

First Yearling Edition 2011

Random House Children's Books supports the First Amendment and celebrates the right to read.

To the other members of our critique group—
Betsy Kraft, Laura Melmed, Peggy Thomson—
a thousand thanks for their insight, their patience,
and their own marvelous books

CHAPTER ONE

March 6

They'll probably be polite—crisp as a soda cracker on the outside, hard as day-old biscuits underneath.

Papaw says not to prejudice my heart before I've got there. But Miss Dixon says to write down what we think now so we can compare it with what we feel after.

In the weeks I've been worrying on what to put in the old yellow suitcase—used to be Jessie's—I've taken out every last thing and tried another. I think that how I look and what I wear shouldn't matter, but I feel that anything I put on my back will stand out like a new pimple.

Shirl says those folks in Lexington are so blue-blooded that even their snot is blue, but the farthest she's been is up to Hazard or down to Harlan, same as me. We could count on our fingers the times we've been more than ten miles out of Thunder Creek, I'll bet.

Ma and Daddy don't much like me going on this exchange program. If I was still living in their house, they wouldn't let me have a stranger from Lexington staying at our place. But since I'm up the hollow at Papaw Mosley's now, they can't very well complain.

Jessie claims it's not me going to Lexington that bothers her; it's Catherine coming here afterward, and what she'll say about us once she goes back. Howard says the same, but he wants to see what Catherine Combs will do when she meets her first copperhead up on the spur.

We were all waiting for Mammaw Mosley's voice on it, because after I come back from Lexington, Catherine will be staying here for two weeks, sleeping with me in my room and eating Mosley food. If Mammaw didn't want the work and worry of another girl around, that would be the end of it, because she's already got Grandmommy to care for.

"Ivy June," she says, "this may be your one chance to see what the rest of the world is like." (Not taking Africa and China into account, of

2

course). But if Lexington's all I'm going to get, I figure I'll take it. And I've got to remember to write about it every blessed day, which is part of the program. Catherine has to keep a journal too. We're supposed to sign our names after each writing, even if we never show our journals to anyone, because putting our name on paper helps us own up to how we feel.

The hardest part will be keeping my mind open and my mouth shut.

Ivy June Mosley

CHAPTER TWO

It was called spring vacation in other parts of the country but mud vacation here in Thunder Creek. The highway that bypassed the valley was paved, but the narrow roads branching off it were dirt. When the rains came, creeks and roads merged in places to become mud, then soup. All but Coal Mine Road, which was asphalt so that the big trucks didn't get stuck. Twenty or more came down that road in a single day.

Ivy June stared at the big calendar on the wall beneath the classroom clock. There were pictures of Egypt for every month. The picture for March was the pyramids, golden as the sand around them. The only connection to Kentucky that Ivy June could see was that the pyramids must have seemed like mountains to people who lived in the desert. To the people of

Cumberland Gap, the huge formations that rose from the earth around them didn't just seem like mountains: they *were*.

Shirley Gaines was studying the map rolled down in front of the blackboard. The assignment had been to plan the routes that Ivy June would take to Lexington if she went by road, by air, and by water. The students were to name the airport nearest to Thunder Creek, and the series of rivers and roads leading north; to determine which routes were even possible; and to figure the cost of going all three ways.

Ivy June watched in amusement as her friend traced a winding blue water line with her finger. The Middle Fork turned and twisted so that Shirl was practically standing on her head as she followed it. By the time her finger got to Beattyville, she was off course and heading for Gray Hawk.

"Shirley, you missed a turn there somewhere, and you're bound for Tennessee," Miss Dixon said.

And Shirl, ever the cutup, whirled herself around and pretended to paddle as fast as she could in the opposite direction. The class roared.

Best friends, Ivy June and Shirley were sometimes mistaken for sisters. Same high cheekbones; same gray eyes, a bit on the squinty side, Shirl's in particular. Same blondish brown hair, strong arms, and skinny legs.

But it was Ivy June who was going on the student exchange with Buckner Academy near Lexington, and if

Shirl was envious, she covered it with antics at the black-board.

⚬⚬⚬

To Ivy June, it seemed as though this last day before mud vacation was a bit more about the exchange program than she would have liked. She was proud, but embarrassed by all the attention. The worst thing you could be here in the mountains was a swelled head. Next to being preg-nant without a husband, maybe.

In seventh-grade social studies the topic was stereo-types. Miss Dixon, who taught three subjects, asked if anyone could think of a stereotype for the bluegrass peo-ple of Kentucky—the horse people.

"Stuck-up and snotty," said Shirl, again to laughter.

"Rich and spoiled," said Fred Mason. "Everyone drives a Mercedes and owns a swimming pool."

"Ha!" said Donald Coates. "Everyone owns a race-track!" More laughter.

"Ivy June?" said the teacher. "Can you give us a stereotype?"

"They think their ideas are the best 'cause their granddaddy was . . . was Thomas Charles Harrison Caldwell the Third or something," said Ivy June, knowing she'd have to write this down in her journal. The class laughed some more. Every single thing she thought and said, almost, had to go in that journal. Her only consola-tion was that Catherine Combs had to do the same.

Miss Dixon only smiled. "Luke," she continued, "what about you?"

And the large boy in the frayed sweatshirt answered, "Everyone's a millionaire and don't even know how to cut his own grass."

"Well, we'll see what Ivy June has to tell us when she gets back," Miss Dixon said, "and of course, we'll get to meet the girl from Buckner Academy ourselves."

Ivy June felt a touch of sympathy for Catherine Combs just then, coming here with all that said against her. But it was Luke's remark that rang in her ears. Last summer, Luke Weller and his brothers had had to get up at five o'clock six days a week to cut grass for a lawn company up north—no vacation at all. And Ivy June truly believed that if anything happened to Papaw while she was away in Lexington, it was because of what she had made happen to Luke Weller's dad.

⁂

At three o'clock Ivy June thrust her arms through the straps of her backpack and glanced furtively down the hall, hoping that Jimmy Harris might come along to tell her goodbye. The eighth graders usually kept to the other end of the building, though, and this day was no exception. Ivy June wondered if she only imagined that his eyes followed her in the cafeteria, and that when he did happen to meet her in the hall, his smile seemed especially friendly.

But Miss Dixon was coming down the corridor instead, the sleeves of her pink sweater pushed up to the elbows. She was the one teacher in middle school who truly looked good in jeans, Ivy June thought. Miss Dixon smiled as she tucked an envelope into the side pocket of the backpack.

"The teachers wanted you to have a little spending money when you go to Lexington," she said. "It's not much, but it might come in handy."

Ivy June didn't know if it would be more polite to accept or refuse it. "Well . . . thank you," she said, surprised. "You didn't have to. . . ."

"No, but we wanted to," Miss Dixon said, giving Ivy June's arm a squeeze. "After all, you're our ambassador, remember."

Ivy June gave her a shy smile. "Thanks a lot," she said.

On the bus, she slid in beside Shirl and put her backpack on the floor between her feet.

"What was Miss Dixon saying to you?" Shirl asked.

Ivy June tried not to smile. "Called me an ambassador."

"Huh! I've called you a lot of names in my life, but I never called you that," Shirl joked. She dug in her bag for a small pocket dictionary and thumbed through the "A" pages. " 'Ambassador,' " she read. " 'An official envoy. A diplomatic agent of the highest rank.' " She turned to Ivy June. "It means you stink."

"Does *not!*"

"Does!" Shirley flipped through the pages to "R" and looked up "rank," then held it out for Ivy June to see. " 'Offensive in odor. Offensively gross.' "

Ivy June laughed and gave her a shove. "Anyway," she said, unzipping the pocket of her backpack, "she gave me an envelope."

"Yeah? A going-away card? Bet there's a ten-dollar bill," said Shirl.

Ivy June took out the envelope. She found a congratulations card inside, along with two twenties. Shirley whistled. Ivy June could scarcely believe it.

With every good wish for a remarkable journey, the message read, and all the teachers had signed it.

"Wow! Two weeks in Lexington and two twenties besides?" said Shirl, this time letting the envy show.

"You should have put your name in for the exchange program," Ivy June said. "Might have been you who was going."

"Yeah, but last thing in this world I'd want is one of those Academy girls staying with *me* for two weeks after I got back," Shirl told her. "And Pa wouldn't hear of it." Which meant that she'd tried.

The fact was that when the invitation had come from the Buckner Academy for Girls to participate in a seventh-grade student exchange, the teachers at Thunder Creek Middle School had decided that any seventh-grade girl could submit her name. But she had to bring a note from home saying that the family was able and willing to take on a guest for two weeks. Ivy June had supposed that at least half the seventh-grade girls would turn in notes the next day, but at the end of the week, only six families had said they were willing. After a teacher's visit to each of those homes, the names had been placed in a coffee can and shaken around. The principal herself had drawn the winning name: Ivy June Mosley.

As the bus bounced along the pockmarked road that rimmed Parson's Gap, Ivy June looked for signs of spring in the still-desolate landscape. The state road led up into the mountains, where all roads leading off it were even narrower. Like the limbs of a tree, there were branches off branches, and most of them were wet and rutted. The bus stuck to the main route. At each stop its passengers had to hike the rest of the distance home themselves.

White leafless birches stood out like skeleton trees, their bones spread-eagled against a backdrop of pine. *At the end—you meet God* was carved into a wooden post, almost obscured by the brown vines of kudzu that covered tree and bush as far as Ivy June could see. One day the kudzu looked like wire strung out over the landscape, and the next it would be green and leafy once again.

As the bus maneuvered a switchback, Shirl asked, "What time do you leave tomorrow?"

"Papaw's driving me to Hazard at eleven. That's where the Academy folks will pick me up," Ivy June told her.

"Scared?" asked Shirl, her squinty eyes studying Ivy June closely.

"Why should I be?" asked Ivy June, wondering if Shirl could read her face.

Shirl shrugged. "No particular reason. Hope you don't have to spend the whole vacation being their maid or something."

"You're crazy," Ivy June told her. "It'll be fun."

Shirl gave her a mischievous grin. "You'll miss me, though."

"Sure I will. But you won't miss me. You'll be too busy kissing Fred Mason."

"I *never!*" Shirl objected, punching Ivy June's arm, then laughed.

Ivy June laughed too and stood up as the bus came to a stop at a tiny roadside shack not much bigger than a phone booth. Two or even three children could squeeze into it while they waited for a bus in bad weather. Elementary school buses, for grades one through six, stopped there first, and Ivy June's eight-year-old brother, Ezra, always headed home as soon as he got off, eager for a snack. But Howard liked to fool around. Today he was poking a long stick at a winter-dazed toad in the weeds. One year younger than Ivy June, Howard was already an inch taller; he was growing lankier by the day, and his feet seemed too big for his body. He grinned as he watched Ivy June climb down off the bus.

"Who-eee!" he called, glad for vacation. "Won't have to ride the bus for nine whole days!" As the bus moved on, he said, "Me and Kenny's got this wood wagon, you know? And we found this old bike? And we took off the handlebars?"

He and Ivy June started up the narrow side road that ran along a creek.

"Yeah? What are you fixing to do?" Ivy June asked.

"Make a go-cart or something. See if we can't hook up a motor to it."

"Where are you going to get a motor, Howard Paul?"

"Lawn mower, maybe."

"And what are you going to do for gas?" Ivy June demanded. She looked over at the toad that Howard held out in front of him, wedged now between the ends of two sticks. "You thinking of siphoning any gas out of Daddy's pickup, he'll kill you."

"Wouldn't take much," said Howard, tipping the sticks one way, then the other, as though he were toasting a marshmallow.

"Howard, quit worrying that toad and listen to me," Ivy June said. "Ma's going to need your help while I'm gone. Don't you be off with Kenny Holland all the time."

"She won't need me more'n she ever did. You're not around that much anyway," said Howard, letting the toad go free.

It stung. "I'm around enough to help out now and then," Ivy June said. "I'm only a spit away at Mammaw's, and don't think I don't have work to do there."

"So, I'm around too!" said Howard.

"If you're not off breaking your neck on some go-cart,"

said Ivy June. They trudged on up the road, skirting the puddles.

Howard glanced over at her. "You really want to do this? Go off up there, don't even know anybody?"

"Yes! I really want to!"

"Bet they're just waitin' to pull some mean trick on you, make everybody laugh."

"You only think that because you've got ideas of your own when Catherine comes here," Ivy June said, then regretted that she was arguing with one of her three brothers on her last afternoon home. "Anyway," she said, "Mammaw and I made an apple cake last night for you all to eat over vacation."

Howard's eyes lit up. "The kind with holes poked on top and brown sugar syrup poured through?"

"Yep," said Ivy June. "She's got it there on the shelf— said you could come up and get it this afternoon."

Howard's feet picked up speed. "Tell Ma I'm off to get the cake," he said, and hurried on ahead.

Each day after school, Ivy June stopped in first to check with Ma—see if there was anything needed— before going on up the hollow to her grandparents'. She didn't have to do this, but she felt obliged. It was Ivy June, after all, whom Mammaw and Papaw had chosen to live with them a year ago when her own house had gotten too crowded.

When Danny was born, that had made five kids in the family, counting nineteen-year-old Jessie. The two girls

13

had shared one bedroom, their parents and Danny another, while Howard and Ezra had taken turns, one on the couch, the other on the floor. With Ivy June at her grandparents', Ma had been able to fix up the tiny back room off the kitchen just for Jessie, so that all three boys could sleep in the room the girls used to share.

So why didn't she get the same welcome in the house she'd left that she got at Mammaw's? Ivy June wondered. It was as though she'd moved ten miles away. Why wasn't the family glad that her leaving had meant more space for the rest of them? Why did Jessie seem so resentful lately, and Ma have a frown on her face when Ivy June came by after school?

"I didn't ask to go live at Mammaw's. She and Papaw invited me," Ivy June reminded herself. But down deep she knew the real reason her parents and siblings were chilly toward her: she had been offered the chance to go to Lexington and she'd taken it. She was going to stay in the kind of house you only saw in magazines and mix with the kind of people who worked in offices, not mines. For two weeks she was going to attend a private school with girls who didn't wear their sisters' hand-me-downs. And that made the distance between Ivy June's old house and Papaw and Mammaw's seem greater still.

CHAPTER THREE

March 7

   I'm supposed to write down what I expect Ivy
June and her family to be like, so I can compare
it with my impressions after I get to know them.
   I'm excited I was chosen for this project. Even
more excited to have someone my own age in the
house. It'll be like one long sleepover. But the
assignment assumes I have these stereotypes or
prejudices against people who live a lot more
simply than we do, and I'd like to think I don't.
   Mom and Dad say it will be a great experience,
Ivy June coming here for two weeks and then me
going there. The twins are mostly curious. Rosemary
says these projects sound good at the beginning but

don't usually turn out like they're supposed to, and that they end up making the poor resent the rich. I don't see us as rich, but Rosemary's been on my case ever since she married Grandpa. If she doesn't argue about one thing, it's another. At least she and Gramps live across town, not with us. That's one thing to be grateful for.

I'm ready for anything. I've gone camping a lot, so I can do without luxuries when I go to Thunder Creek, and I know exactly what an outhouse is. Peter had to describe one for Claire, and she screamed "Ewwww!" I hope they don't embarrass Ivy June by asking her about it when she comes.

What if she hates the city or gets homesick or can't do some of the assignments at school? What if I get homesick when I go there? What if I find them strange? I think I can handle it, though.

Here's what I expect the Mosleys will be like: sort of hard to get to know at first, but they'll tell me just what they think if I ask their opinion about something. They'll be easily offended if they feel I'm putting them down. And it's probably true that they're mistrustful of outsiders and want to stick to tradition. Are these stereotypes? Maybe. (I'm glad I don't have to show this journal to anyone unless I want to.)

Mom says we'll do everything we can to make Ivy June feel welcome. I told her the best way we can do that is to lock Rosemary in the basement if she visits. (If you're reading this, Rosemary, I'm joking! I'm joking! And you know you're not supposed to be snooping in my stuff.)

Catherine Combs

CHAPTER FOUR

As Ivy June trudged along the narrow dirt road, the wall of rock on her right grew higher and steeper; the creek on her left grew wider. On up ahead she could hear Howard's footsteps on the planks of the swinging bridge, which had a cable along one side as a handrail. A misty rain was falling, just enough for her to feel on her face. It had been raining on and off for a week, and from the gray look of the sky, it would go on raining forever.

As Ivy June rounded the bend, her eyes checked the small clearing beside the bridge. Jessie's car would be there, of course, unless she'd left early for her shift at the sweatshirt factory. What Ivy June didn't want to see was her father's pickup, which would mean he hadn't found enough work to keep him away till sundown. What she did want to see was Papaw's dusty blue Chevy, which would mean he was home from the mine, safe for another day. This time both her daddy's pickup and the old Chevy were in the clearing, so they sort of canceled each other out.

Ivy June stepped onto the bridge, and it swayed as she walked. Each footstep made a hollow thunking sound, and after nine steps she was walking toward the little frame house with its covered front porch, a single window on each side of the door. In back, Daddy was splitting wood and stacking it on the pile.

Ivy June went around the house.

"Papaw's driving me to Hazard tomorrow, so I came to say goodbye," she said.

It was Papaw letting her go, so Papaw's gas was getting her there.

Russell Mosley glanced her way momentarily, then lifted the sledgehammer again and brought it down on the iron wedge with a clank.

"You all set, then?" he asked, reaching down to toss the splintered chunks to one side.

"Just have to close my suitcase," Ivy June told him.

"Well then," he said, and after another silence added, "Supposed to rain all week. Good you're outta here before the road turns mud."

He was a man of few words, her daddy. Tall and thin, with a sallow look about his face. After two or three swings of the sledgehammer, he'd stop to rest a bit, leaning on the end of the handle. Any day he felt up to it, he

19

was out driving around picking up scrap metal for a company that bought aluminum. If he was lucky, he was doing carpentry work. But a carpenter's job was hard to come by.

"If ever there was a hard-luck boy, it was Russell," Mammaw told Ivy June once. "Like the runt in a litter, he was always the sickly one. Asthma and allergies . . . Had the fever when he was twelve, and we thought we were going to lose him then. But he hung on and growed up to marry your mama. Ruth don't like it here, but at least they're close by. Long as we got legs and our backs don't give out, your grandpa and I can grow food enough for all of us."

Ivy June watched her daddy now. It was probably difficult for him to feel good about himself when he had to depend on someone else, and his own job didn't even have a name to it. Handyman came closest, but there wasn't enough outside work to fill more than a day or two a week.

"Well," she said finally, shifting to her other foot. "I'll probably write a postcard or two."

"We'll look for 'em," her daddy said, and gave her a little smile.

She'd never been away from home for more than a night. For a moment she considered walking around the pile of wood chips and giving her daddy a hug. But his arms didn't offer, so her feet didn't move. She gave him a small smile back and went on inside.

〰

As Ivy June stepped onto the worn linoleum, she heard her mother's voice from beyond the kitchen:

"Hold up that end, Jessie, if you want those curtains to hang straight. I can't use the hammer and keep up both ends myself." Seeing Ivy June, she said sharply, "Can't you give us a hand?"

Ivy June slid the backpack off her shoulder and entered the tiny room, more like a pantry. There was scarcely enough space for the single bed and a dresser, though a straight-backed chair had been crammed in one corner. "What you want me to do?"

"Give me a couple those nails on the bed there, and tell me if this rod is straight," said her mother. "Saw these in the Penney's catalog, half price, so we got us a pair."

Ivy June handed her the nails and stepped back a little. "Raise up your end about an inch, Jessie," she said. "Now down a little. Yeah. Right about there."

Ruth Mosley began to pound, then handed the hammer to Jessie—Jessie with the dark hair and high cheekbones.

"Looks nice," Ivy June said, over the pounding. "The green matches the squares in the quilt." One of Grandmommy's quilts, of course, from back when she could still sew.

"Well, it's not a Lexington bedroom, but at least I've got it to myself," said Jessie as she and her mother worked to even out the folds of the curtain.

There was that tone again. Jessie couldn't seem to say the word "Lexington" without it. And the fact that both her mother and Jessie had their backs to her gave Ivy June the courage to say, "You've had this room for a year, Jessie.

What are you angry about now? That I'm going to Lexington?"

Jessie turned around. "Why should I be angry?" She reached for the sweater she'd tossed on the bed. "I just think it's a dumb idea, is all. You're like to feel you're living in a hotel, and when that Academy girl gets here, she's going to feel like she's anywhere but."

"You don't know what I'll feel, or Catherine, either!" Ivy June said hotly.

Ruth Mosley stepped down off the box where she'd been standing, her voice more gentle. "What she's sayin', Ivy June, is don't be tryin' to rise above your raisin'. We're not ever likely to have the things they've got up in Lexington, and why your Mammaw and Papaw thought it was a good idea for you to go up there is more than I can figure."

"This isn't about 'things,' it's about meeting new people and seeing new places and getting new ideas, is all," said Ivy June. "I'm not looking for 'things.'"

Her mother grunted, gathering up the remaining nails and dropping them in the pocket of her baggy sweatpants. "Well, whether you're lookin' or not, you'll see 'em," she said. "And there's plenty of 'things' we need here we're not ever goin' to have. I'm not lookin' for no diamond ring—just the money to pay the electric and some seed money, but they don't have to worry about that up in Lexington."

Ivy June reached down for her backpack and silently

pulled out the envelope, removing the congratulations card. She handed the envelope to her mother.

"Well then, here," she said. "This is for you . . . while I'm away."

Ruth Mosley looked inside the envelope and stared at the bills, then slowly pulled them out. "What's this?"

"Just something they gave me for Lexington, but I don't need it," Ivy June told her.

"Forty dollars?" Jessie exclaimed.

"Who give you this, Ivy June?" her mother demanded.

"Miss Dixon and the other teachers wanted me to have some spending money, but I already got me some saved up," Ivy June said, knowing it wasn't more than twelve or thirteen dollars.

"Then you shouldn't have took this!" her mother said. "We're not poor folk dependin' on handouts."

"They didn't say I was poor, Ma," Ivy June told her. "They said I was the ambassador for their school, *that's* what they called me."

Mrs. Mosley studied her daughter for a moment, then looked down at the money in her hand.

"They *wanted* her to have it, Ma, so keep it!" Jessie said impatiently.

Mrs. Mosley's face softened. "You're sure you don't need this, Ivy June?"

"One hundred percent positive," Ivy June declared.

There were hurried footsteps on the porch; then the door banged open as Howard came in, bringing the apple cake, his two younger brothers at his heels—Ezra, with his round cheeks, and three-year-old Danny, dressed in his hand-me-downs.

"Mammaw sent us down her apple cake!" Howard chortled. "Her and Ivy June made it."

"Can we have a piece now?" begged Ezra, one finger poised to scoop up the syrup around the edge of the platter.

"And me!" said Danny, crawling up on a kitchen chair.

Ruth Mosley tucked the two twenties into her pocket and smiled. "Yes, we'll all of us have a piece right now. Go get your daddy, Ezra. Set down, Ivy June, and let's celebrate."

CHAPTER FIVE

A pair of gray flannel long johns jiggled and flapped in the wind like an old man trying to dance. The heavier items, the overalls and sheets strung on a line across Mammaw's front porch, tried to resist the gusts that blew through the hollow.

As Ivy June approached her grandparents' house, she thought about how the babbling water in Thunder Creek would soon become a loud rush; it would be the last thing they'd hear before falling asleep at night, the first sound to greet them in the morning. Every spring the questions were the same: would the water get as high as the footbridge, and would it flood the road? Flooding was something Papaw had to consider every morning when he left for work at the mine.

By the time Catherine Combs came in April, however,

the shadbush and wild honeysuckle would be in bloom, and every day the sun would reach the valley floor a little sooner. It was nice in the mountains then, and there was nowhere Ivy June would rather be.

She missed the wagging welcome of old Nancy, Papaw's dog, a loving, protective black-and-white mutt that never skipped a chance to lick your hand. They'd lost her over the winter—she'd been older than Ivy June.

Now, as Ivy June went up the steps of the frame house, only the two cats were there, huddled down on chairs. A damp sheet obscured the washing machine that sat next to the rocker, and she had to duck under a towel to get inside the door. She made her way back to the kitchen, where the fragrant smell of stewed chicken met her nostrils.

"And dumplings?" she asked, grinning at Mammaw.

The thin little woman with the gray braid around her head smiled, still stirring. "Figured you ought to get all your favorites, your last night here."

"You make it sound like execution day," Ivy June said, and slipped her arms around her grandmother, hugging her from behind. "I'll never get chicken and dumplings up there."

Mammaw reached back and poked her affectionately. "Don't be makin' up your mind about things in advance, Ivy June. Pray they *don't* live the same as we do, or what's the point a goin' a'tall?"

Ivy June dropped her backpack on a chair. "I'm going

to miss you," she said, studying her grandmother's faded print dress, her full apron that slipped over her head, and her two spindly legs, which ended with white canvas Keds on her feet.

"Not as much as we'll miss you, honey," Mammaw said.

There was the sound of water splashing on the enclosed back porch—Papaw washing up. He would get the worst of the coal dust off when he showered at the mine, but it took another scrubbing when he got home, he said, to get rid of the second layer.

"Water ready?" he'd ask, opening the door from the back porch, where he'd piled his dirty clothes, and Mammaw would carry the teakettle out and fill the basin next to the pump. The coveralls, the boots, the work shirt and helmet were left at the mine, hanging high overhead in the locker room to dry. But the grime even coated the clothes he wore underneath, and he changed once again before dinner.

Ivy June could remember the mine where Papaw had worked before; it had had no shower at all. She could remember his passing their house on his way up the hill when he came home—the way the coal dust had so blackened the lines on either side of his mouth and the wrinkles in his neck that she couldn't understand how he would ever get it out. In some places he couldn't. Even now it filled the space beneath his fingernails, as well as the deep crinkles at the corners of his eyes.

Ivy June loved this time of day—the security of having

Papaw home, the sound of sloshing water back on the porch. Once in a while Papaw whistled as he scrubbed. Occasionally he even hummed. She wondered sometimes if she felt closer to her grandparents than she'd ever felt to her parents. Yet when Papaw and Mammaw had been raising their six boys, perhaps they'd had no more time to spare than Ma and Daddy did for her. Whatever the reason, she loved that special feeling of being the only child here.

Ivy June and Mammaw wouldn't see Papaw again until he entered the kitchen in his twill trousers and flannel shirt, his weathered neck red from scrubbing. Then he'd take his glass of cider into the parlor and sit by the coal stove, letting his stocking feet recover from the confines of his knee-high rubber boots.

Ivy June set about her daily chores. If there wasn't enough kindling in the wood box by the iron stove, then Mammaw would have to go out to the woodpile herself. If Ivy June didn't empty Grandmommy's chamber pot, you could smell it along about mealtime. If she didn't feed the cats, they'd be meowing and scratching at the back door for scraps, and if she didn't keep up with the dust in the parlor, either Mammaw or Grandmommy would get to sneezing.

"I got time before supper, or is there something else you need me to do?" Ivy June asked when she'd completed her work.

"It'll be a while yet," said Mammaw. "You wrap up those jars of preserves you're taking?"

"Three layers of newspaper each," said Ivy June.

"Then you can go say your goodbye to the mountains," Mammaw told her.

It was as though her head were made of glass and her grandmother could see through it, Ivy June thought as she set out up the winding path to the Whistling Place. It was not Ivy June or Papaw who whistled there. It was the wind. A quarter mile up that path, there was a jutting-out spur of land overlooking the hollow, with a steep wall of rock behind it. Three thin saplings grew so close to the rock that when the wind came through, it made a rushing, whistling sound.

The saplings grew between the rock wall and a flat, raised boulder, and Ivy June marveled that they grew at all. They reminded her of the plaque in Mammaw's kitchen, just above the stove: BLOOM WHERE YOU ARE PLANTED, it read. And those trees did just that.

Ivy June crawled up on the flat boulder, surveying the valley below, and gulped back a welling-up of homesickness that took her by surprise. She'd not set foot off the mountain yet, and she was missing it already. It was a place she came to often, sometimes to sing, accompanied by the wind, and sometimes with her sketch pad. Once she drew only a close-up of a branch. Another time she sketched the clouds. She drew Papaw's house below, from this angle or that. Last fall she had taken one of those sketches to art class at school and she'd used watercolors to fill it in, squinting as she worked, so that she painted it as it might appear through mist or fog, the edges blurred. Mrs. Sullivan had liked it so much she'd found a frame for it, and Ivy June had presented it to her mother.

Mrs. Mosley had studied it a little, holding it out away from her. "It's Papaw's house, all right, Ivy June," she had said, "but it looks to be out of focus."

"Just another way of painting, Ma. I wanted to try something new," Ivy June told her.

Howard had said, "Why didn't you just take a picture of it?"

And Jessie had commented, "I want to hang a picture of a house on my wall, I'll cut one out of a magazine or something."

When it had lain around for a week or two and no one had volunteered to put it up, Ivy June had taken it to Papaw's house and hung it on the wall in her own small bedroom.

⚬⚬⚬

When she got back from the Whistling Place, Papaw was napping in his chair in the parlor.

"Grandmommy's awake now," Mammaw said. "Go in there and see if you can entertain her till supper, will you? Read her that birthday card she got last week."

"I've only read it a dozen times!" Ivy June said.

"Well, make that thirteen, then. She never tires of it, you doing the reading." The small dining room had been converted to a bedroom, with a daybed, a wheelchair, and

30

an array of bottles and ointments on a low shelf along with a Bible, a brush, and Grandmommy's figurines.

The tiny woman sat immobile in the wheelchair, her feet in mended stockings, her toes barely reaching the footrest. Her scalp showed pink beneath the white strands of hair, and her fingers were knobby at the joints, veins standing out raised and blue on the backs of her hands like the rivers on the map of Kentucky.

It was hard to know how much Grandmommy could see, because both eyes were cloudy. But she always seemed to know when Ivy June was there.

"Well!" she said, turning her head and smiling as Ivy June leaned down to kiss her cheek.

"How you doing, Grandmommy?" Ivy June asked, sitting on the edge of the daybed.

The old woman managed a smile but didn't answer.

"What'll it be this afternoon? The Bible? The almanac?" Ivy June asked.

In answer, Grandmommy jiggled a large white card in her lap, and Ivy June dutifully took it from her wrinkled fingers and began reading aloud from the top:

"From the White House: Dear Mrs. Mosley, Please accept our heartfelt congratulations on the occasion of your one hundredth birthday. . . ."

"Just cain't . . . understand . . . how the President knew . . . about my birthday," Grandmommy interrupted, as Ivy June knew she would. Ivy June would never tell her that one of Kentucky's senators forwarded names to the

White House if anyone let him know of a Kentucky resident who had reached the century mark.

" 'Cause you're special, and everybody around here loves you," said Ivy June.

The old woman moistened her lips and said something else, but Ivy June had to lean down to hear.

"Almost all the friends I had . . . are gone," said Grandmommy, her voice wavery as a loose string.

"Well, you got us, and all of them down at the house. That's nine right there," said Ivy June, and continued reading:

"How wonderful to know that you have lived to see some of the greatest scientific advancements in human history—the discovery of penicillin, man's walk on the moon—"

"I never did," the old woman interrupted again.

"Never did what?" asked Ivy June.

"Believe that. About the moon," said Grandmommy. "It's like . . . in the Bible, you know . . . the Tower of Babel. Men tried it before, and . . . God stopped 'em short. Never meant it t'happen."

Ivy June had to smile. "But the Bible's full of miracles. You believe in miracles, don't you?"

"Walkin' on the moon . . . was no miracle," said Grandmommy, "and no science, neither. It's hogwash." She raised her head defiantly. "Now go on. . . ."

Ivy June continued to read.

In the evenings, if he wasn't too tired to talk, Papaw

was full of stories, and generous with his smiles. There was always a smile on his face when Ivy June came in. She was his favorite grandchild, and she knew it.

But he also made time for the others. She remembered once when they'd all been playing up here at Papaw's and hadn't set out for home till after dark. Ezra, not quite seven at the time, had been afraid of the shadows and all the night sounds, and Papaw had walked them the four hundred or so yards back to the house.

Holding little Danny's hand on one side of him, Ezra's on the other, Papaw had said, "Why, boy, you don't know what dark is. Up here you got the stars, you got the fireflies, you got the light down in your ma's kitchen—I can see it from here. Down in the mine, you turn off your carbide lamp and it's black as black can be. You can't even imagine anythin' that dark."

"But it don't make scary sounds!" Ezra put in as crickets chirped around them and an old hoot owl picked that time to cut loose.

"You kiddin' me?" Papaw said. "You go way deep in a mountain, turn off the machines for a minute, and you can't imagine the sounds. The mountain groans and it shifts, like a giant movin' around in his chair. It's a noise like a handful of marbles rubbin' together. You'd never think a mountain would talk to you, but you go down six hundred feet, you'll believe it."

Ivy June knew, from hearing this story before, that this was the time the tunnel roof had caved in and Papaw and the other miners had waited all night to be rescued. All night, sitting in the dark, listening to rock shift and moan. But when Danny and Ezra were around, Papaw never talked about danger. That was something he kept to himself.

Then he had picked up Danny and pointed out Venus, the brightest star in the sky. "We see a light like that down in the mine," he said, "why, it'd be like the sun to us. It's not dark up here, Ezra. You got all the stars, all the fireflies lightin' your way home."

And what Ivy June remembered most about that night was not the stars or fireflies but the thought of Papaw, six hundred feet down, in the dark.

The mine where Papaw worked now was a drift mine. The entrance was a big yawning hole in the side of the mountain, and mine cars carried the men a mile or two straight in. But whether Papaw went two miles in or six hundred feet down, he was surrounded by rock, and that was something Ivy June could not forget.

On this particular night, however—Ivy June's last dinner at home—Papaw's smile was wider than ever when he came to the table, and just as Ivy June was about to kid him that it must be because she was leaving, he said, "Four more months and I retire, Ivy June. What do you think of that?"

"And you won't ever have to go back in the mine again?" she asked. "Not even if they're short of men?"

"Not ever. Once I step off that mine car, it's the last

I'll set foot on it again." He took another swallow of cider and set the glass on the table, savoring the array of food spread out before him—the homegrown green beans, pickled beets with onions, corn bread and sweet butter, and of course, the chicken.

Mammaw smiled too as she wheeled Grandmommy up to the table and tied a dish towel around her neck. "That will sure be some happy day!" she said. "Wonder how you ever made it through, Spencer. Sometimes you'd get so disgusted with life you couldn't see what was ahead and what was behind, but it didn't stop you." She leaned down and planted a kiss on his weathered cheek.

Ivy June buttered Grandmommy's corn bread for her. "What are you going to do, Papaw, when you don't have to get up at four and drive all the way to the mine?" she asked.

The tall man with the crinkles about the eyes grinned as he helped himself to the chicken. "Well, for the first year, I'll wake up at four out of habit. Take me another year to learn to walk upright, not bent over like an ape. Third year I'll still be washin' coal dust out of my creases, and maybe by year four, I'll see if there's any more fish left in the creek."

Mammaw laughed out loud at this, but Grandmommy smacked her toothless gums together and said, "He just . . . wouldn't listen. Wouldn't . . . listen a'tall."

And everyone at the table knew she was talking about her husband, Papaw's daddy, who had gone to work in the

35

mine despite Grandmommy's pleas for him to find factory work, and had gotten so much coal dust in his lungs he never lived to retire.

"Here, Iree," Mammaw said, mashing some beans with the back of her spoon and holding them to the old woman's mouth.

But Grandmommy was looking in Papaw's direction, and Ivy June knew her great-grandma wouldn't rest easy—none of them would—till he was out of the mine for good.

CHAPTER SIX

March 8

Hard to sleep last night. When rain hits the tin roof, it sounds like acorns coming down. If the road floods while I'm gone, Papaw's going to have to take the long way home, park up at Vulture Pass, and walk down through there.

I've got a homesickness growing inside me already for Papaw and Mammaw, and even a little for Grandmommy. But the lonesomeness I've got for Ma and Daddy is more like for what I wish they were, and that's hard to put down on paper. I know what their worry's done to them, though, and I figure we all love each other down underneath where you can't hardly see it.

But it wasn't the rain that kept me awake, and not excitement, either, though that's part of it. It's the same thing that's upset my sleep for the past thirteen months—the memory of what I did to Luke Weller's family.

The closest I ever came to telling anybody was when I let Papaw know once how worried I was about him when he was in the mine. And the next night he came home, he called me out on the porch, his face all grimy with coal dust, and he says, "Got something for you." He gives me this little piece of rock. It's about as big as a walnut, smooth on one side, rough on the other.

"This is from way back in the mine," he tells me. "A million years old or more. You keep it somewheres, Ivy June, and whenever you get to worrying, you just take this rock and hold it in your hand. Tell yourself that your Papaw's as strong and hard as that old rock. It can shatter, it's true, but it would take a mighty blow, and it's the same with me."

So I've packed that rock in my suitcase. But not even Papaw knows what I once asked God to do, and that's a sin I've got to carry along with me.

Ivy June Mosley

CHAPTER SEVEN

March 8

When you don't know someone at all, it's hardest not to make a mistake. All I really know about Ivy June is her name and where she's from. We're supposed to collect all the rest of the information ourselves after our exchange student gets here—a way of getting to know her, I suppose. This is scary! So I asked Mackenzie and Hannah for their expert opinions, and they started right off with clothes.

"It's okay to offer her a school uniform, but forget the socks," Hannah told me.

"Definitely forget the socks," said Mackenzie. "Explain to her that she's a guest, and she can wear whatever she wants."

I worry a lot about offending Ivy June in some way. Mackenzie said, "Wow! Two whole weeks! You're brave, Cat! I wouldn't even want a cousin hanging around for two weeks." And Rosemary doesn't help either.

She calls the exchange program a "disaster in the making."

"It'll be fine," said Hannah. "You'll go down in our school's history as the first exchange student with Thunder Creek. Just remember that whatever Ivy June is like, she could have been a tattoo artist or a snake handler or something." There are those stereotypes again. But stereotypes always start from something, don't they?

Right now I'm sitting in the living room writing this in my journal while Peter and Claire run to the window every time they hear a car. I hope Ivy June has a ten-year-old brother or sister, because she's sure going to see enough of the twins while—

She's here! Peter and Claire are already at the door. I'm hoping that, like Mrs. Fields says, these next two weeks will be two of the most important in my life, and not—as Rosemary predicts—a waste of spring vacation, and then some.

Catherine Combs

CHAPTER EIGHT

Ivy June climbed out the passenger side of the car, glancing up at the house uncertainly. It was not a movie-star kind of place, but a mayor could have lived there once. A governor, even. *How could a house need so many windows?* she wondered.

Her shoulder bag was slung over one shoulder, and she carried the preserves in a paper bag in one hand. With the other, she opened the rear door and hauled out her yellow suitcase, her body tilting to the left after she picked it up.

Mrs. Fields, the assistant headmistress of Buckner Academy, got out the driver's side and hurried around the car to help, holding an umbrella above her head.

"I can carry it okay," Ivy June said, secretly hoping the latch wouldn't give out and dump all her things in the driveway. She stayed close to Mrs. Fields as they moved up the walk, rain pelting one shoulder. The suitcase bumped awkwardly against Ivy June's leg as they went up the steps and onto the wide porch.

A small crowd was waiting for her just inside the door. The girl her own age, one size larger, perhaps, must be Catherine, Ivy June thought. Two smaller kids were wearing toothy grins.

"Hi, Ivy June," the girl said, smiling. "I'm Catherine. Hello, Mrs. Fields."

Mrs. Fields held out a welcome basket that the Academy had prepared for Ivy June. "Hello, Catherine. I'll let you carry this in for her. Gracious, this certainly is a wet welcome, isn't it? But it was raining even harder down in Hazard."

A woman appeared in the doorway behind the younger children. She was thin-faced and wore a sweater draped around her neck and shoulders.

"Come right in!" she called, smiling. "I'm Mrs. Combs, Ivy June. We're so glad to have you!"

"I've got to run. We're having an anniversary celebration for my parents this evening, and I'm in charge," said Mrs. Fields. "I know the girls want time to get acquainted. It was a pleasure, Ivy June. I'll see you at school on Monday."

Goodbyes were said, Mrs. Fields dashed back to her car, and Ivy June followed Catherine into the large house.

"These are the twins, Peter and Claire," Catherine said, motioning toward the boy and girl. "They've promised to be on their best behavior, but there are no guarantees."

Ivy June laughed then, and the twins grinned some more. She handed the paper bag to Mrs. Combs. "These

42

are for you," she said. "Mammaw sent them." Then, seeing the puzzled look on the woman's face, she added, "My grandmother. She made them."

"Why, thank you!" Mrs. Combs said. She walked into the dining room and set the sack on the table, then lifted out three jars, each wrapped in newspaper. When the wrapping came off, she read the labels, "Elderberry, blackberry, and wild plum. How nice of your grandmother, Ivy June!" she said. "Blackberry is my favorite!"

"Dad's too," Catherine said to Ivy June. "He's working this afternoon, but he'll be here for dinner." And then, when a short, dark-haired woman appeared in the kitchen doorway, Catherine said, "And that's Flora. She's helping out for a few days."

Ivy June hoped she would remember all these names. She and Flora exchanged smiles.

Claire had her eye on the welcome basket. "Let's see what you got!" she said.

"Claire!" said Catherine, but Ivy June smiled and gamely took the basket from her and set it on the table. A few pieces of fruit, some candy bars, and some school mementoes—notebook, pen, paperweight, erasers—all with *Buckner Academy for Girls* printed on them. Ivy June gave the candy bars to the twins, and they accepted, ignoring the reprimand on their mother's face.

"Catherine's going to take you to your room and help you get settled," Mrs. Combs said. "She'll show you around the house so you'll know where everything is. Please tell us if you need anything."

43

"I think I've got everything I need right here, but thank you," Ivy June said, gesturing toward her suitcase.

She followed Catherine up the stairs, the twins close at their heels. A large vase of dried flowers stood on the landing beneath a small window of stained glass. Another half flight of stairs led to the floor above.

There were four doors off the upper hallway.

"This is mine," said Catherine, going into a bedroom with twin beds, each covered with an eyelet spread. Everything in the room was blue and white—the beds, the desk, the lamp and chair—all fitted to one girl's individual taste.

"I can sleep anywhere," Catherine said. "Which bed would you like?"

Ivy June looked around. "The one by the window," she said. "I like the night sounds."

Catherine seemed to hesitate. "Well, I think we can open the windows, but we usually keep them closed because of Peter's allergies."

Ivy June looked amazed. "Even in summer?"

"Oh, we turn on the air," said Catherine, then added quickly, "The air-conditioning."

"It's okay," Ivy June said, and set her suitcase on the floor.

"We'll unpack later, but let me show you around," said Catherine, and walked to a second door off the bedroom. Ivy June made a detour to the window to look down on the street below, then walked over to where Catherine stood.

"Here's our bathroom. We'll share it with Claire—she sleeps in the room on the other side." Then, to her brother, she said, "And remember, Peter, you've got to use Mom and Dad's bathroom while Ivy June's here."

"I *know* that! You don't have to tell me!" Peter replied. He and Claire had dark hair like Catherine's and the same blue eyes and pinched nose as their mother.

Catherine turned to Ivy June again. "The only thing to remember is to lock both doors when you use the bathroom—this one and the one leading to Claire's room."

Ivy June was confused momentarily, and Peter took the opportunity to brush past her in the doorway and point out the handle of the toilet. "You just push down on this, and it'll flush," he said helpfully.

Ivy June saw Catherine's face turn a bright pink. "Peter!" Catherine said, anger in her voice.

Ivy June held back a smile and gave the bathroom a sweeping glance. "You guys don't have a Jacuzzi?" she asked.

Peter stared at her in amazement, and suddenly Catherine and Ivy June broke into laughter. Peter, dumbfounded, sank back into the bedroom.

The twins seemed more cautious of their visitor after that. Catherine pointed out her parents' bedroom next, then Claire's, then Peter's—stocked with more toys and gadgets, it seemed, than a toy store. And everywhere there were books. There were photographs. Family pictures on bedside tables and on walls in the hallway.

Down in the living room again, Ivy June studied bookcases that reached the ceilings. Books on the hearth

45

by the fireplace, stacked under the coffee table. Photos in little leather frames placed in front of the books.

Catherine took her back to view the kitchen, the breakfast nook, then the family room, as well as the laundry room in the basement.

Mr. Combs arrived home just as they were coming upstairs again. He was a large man with broad shoulders and an even broader smile. He gave Ivy June's hand a hearty shake.

"Welcome to the family!" he said. "We hope you'll feel very much at home here, Ivy June."

"Oh, I do already," Ivy June told him, but was glad when she and Catherine could finally escape upstairs to unpack her things. The family seemed to come along with them, however, for one whole wall of Catherine's bedroom held photos for every year of her life: Catherine learning to ride a two-wheeler, Catherine in a speedboat with her dad; Catherine on a sled with the twins; Catherine with her mom at Christmas.

Ivy June tried to remember if there were any photos at all on the walls back at Mammaw's. She could recall only a yellowed photo in a black frame, of Mammaw and Papaw holding the first two of their six children. After that, she imagined, both time to take pictures and money to develop them had grown more scarce. But it must be nice to look up and see a picture of yourself on the wall. To know that somebody liked it enough to put a frame around it and hang it there. Must be nice. . . .

CHAPTER NINE

March 8

My first day in the Combses' house. I'm writing this from a room that looks more like a vanilla ice cream cone than a bedroom. Catherine's in the next bed over, writing in her journal, and I'd give my best pair of shoes to know what she's saying about me. But we promised each other we wouldn't peek.

There's too much I could write—would fill up ten pages. When we got to the library at Hazard, it seemed like Papaw didn't want to hand me over. Like once I left, I'd never come back. Then I gave him a big hug, and I guess that's what he needed.

Now I'm in this huge house—not a palace or

anything, no swimming pool or tennis court. But the laundry room is bigger than the parlor at Mammaw's. You could even put two beds in the hallway at the top of the stairs. I counted four toilets in the house—two on the top floor, one in a "powder room" off the kitchen (no powder in sight), and a toilet in the basement. If five members of the family have to go at the same time, there's only one of them has to wait.

Everyone's friendly enough. Peter reminds me a lot of Howard—says the first thing that comes into his head—and Claire's a funny little thing. Keeps popping up like a jack-in-the-box. So far Catherine's nice as can be. Her ma's getting over the pneumonia, Catherine told me, and has a woman here helping out. Catherine's daddy's big as a bear. Don't know what religion they are, but he did the praying at the table tonight. "Bless it to nourish our good," he says. I just kept my head down and raised it up when everyone else did.

Food was okay, but too rich for my taste. Papaw always says if he can't tell what it is just by looking, he won't like it. Meat in some kind of sauce poured over noodles. And asparagus. That's embarrassing, because it always makes my pee smell funny. But there was pecan pie for dessert, as good as any Mammaw makes.

I'm too sleepy to write more. Having people around all the time, watching me, is a lot more tiring than I expected. Hope I remember to lock both doors when I'm in the bathroom. If I know Claire, she's got one eye at the keyhole anyhow.

Ivy June Mosley

CHAPTER TEN

March 8

Well, we've got Ivy June unpacked and settled
in, and so far things are going okay. We're both
writing in our journals at the moment, since that's
one of the requirements of the program.

She probably thinks we're super rich, and I
suppose we do have a big house for just five people.
I hate to say it, but when Rosemary's around, the
house never seems big enough. I explained to Ivy
June that Mom was really sick a couple of months
ago, and I almost withdrew from the program. But
she's better now, and getting her strength back, and
that's why we have Flora helping out.

I'm not sure what I expected Ivy June to be

wearing, but it's nothing raggedy. No brand-name stuff, of course, but I still think she'd fit in better if she wore the uniform on Monday.

Peter embarrassed me to death explaining the toilet to Ivy June as though she'd never been in a bathroom. I could have wrung his neck. But she's got a sense of humor, and I like that about her. She's pretty quiet, though. It's like she's walking through a jungle and doesn't want to make any sudden moves or noises.

She asked me about school and how much homework she'd be expected to do. I told her just what Mrs. Fields told me, that an exchange student is expected to do as much of each assignment as she can.

I'm hoping Ivy June will be more talkative tomorrow, and feel more comfortable around us. If Peter doesn't try to teach her how to use the remote or something.

Catherine Combs

CHAPTER ELEVEN

Ivy June drifted in and out of sleep, aware, somehow, that it was morning, listening for the sounds of crows bragging to each other in the dead oak down by the footbridge. Listening to hear whether the rush of water was louder now in Thunder Creek, whether there was rain on the tin roof, and whether Papaw was moving about the kitchen, pouring hot coffee into his thermos.

No, she thought, *it's Sunday*, but she heard nothing familiar. No mockingbird doing a warm-up, no sparrows arguing, no blue jay making an announcement . . . only the soft click of a battery-operated wall clock and a car on the street below. Then she remembered and opened her eyes.

Thin lines of daylight came through the slats in the shutters and lay horizontally across the covers. On the bed next to her, Catherine was still asleep, one arm thrown carelessly over her pillow, her head buried somewhere on the other side.

Quietly, Ivy June crawled out of bed, tiptoed to the bathroom, and locked both doors. She used the toilet, brushed her teeth, and filled the sink with hot water, washing up as she did at home when Mammaw poured water from the teakettle into the basin.

When her hair was combed, she remembered to unlock the door leading to Claire's room; then went back to the bedroom and put on clean underwear, the good jeans she'd been wearing the day before, and a yellow knit shirt.

Catherine woke up and rolled over.

"Oh, you're the early one!" she said, sitting up on one elbow. She yawned, then flopped down again. "We don't have to be at church until eleven." She studied Ivy June. "And you don't have to go at all unless you want to. Flora will be here getting dinner, if you'd rather stay. We eat our big meal around noon on Sundays."

Ivy June had already made up her mind that she was going to experience every possible thing she could, so she said, "I'd like to go. What church is it?"

"Methodist." Catherine sat up again. "Are you . . . going to wear that?"

Ivy June glanced down at her shirt and jeans. "I don't know. Shouldn't I?"

"I always wear a dress, but . . . You're fine, really. Unless you want to wear one of mine."

"I've got a dress," Ivy June said quickly, and went to

her suitcase to retrieve the dress she hadn't bothered to unpack. It was a two-piece hand-me-down from Jessie—dark blue polyester with tiny white flowers. It came halfway down to her ankles, the way it was supposed to, but her sneakers looked ridiculous beneath the tiered skirt. Ivy June hauled out the sandals she wore when she dressed up, which was almost never.

Rain slashed at the windows, and she knew that her feet would get wet.

Her stomach growled, but Catherine didn't hear it because she was in the bathroom taking a shower. And after the water turned off, Ivy June could hear the opening and closing of drawers and cabinets, then the whine of a hair dryer.

Lord above, how does she ever get to school on time come Monday? Ivy June thought. She decided to go downstairs, and found Mr. Combs in his robe, reading the Sunday paper at the table. Flora's coat was on a hook by the back door, and she was busily breaking eggs into a bowl.

"Well, look who's up! Good morning!" Mr. Combs said, pulling out another section of paper and sliding the rest toward Ivy June. "More rain, I'm afraid, but next weekend's supposed to be better. What do you like to read at breakfast? Our kids usually start with the comics."

"I don't usually read anything. I've got to feed Grandmommy, anyway," Ivy June said, and sat down.

"Oh. Really?" Mr. Combs said, and lifted his coffee cup again. "How old is your grandmother?"

"My great-grandmother. She was a hundred last month."

54

"A *hundred*?"

Catherine's mother came into the kitchen just then, her hair still loose about her shoulders.

"Did you know that Ivy June's great-grandmother is one hundred years old?" Mr. Combs said.

"My goodness, she must have lived a healthy life!" said Mrs. Combs, easing herself onto one of the chairs.

"Yes, ma'am. If she wasn't sewing quilts, she was out working the garden," Ivy June told her.

"Was she a vegetarian?" asked Mr. Combs.

"She'd eat whatever was on the table," Ivy June said.

"Imagine that." Mrs. Combs accepted the basket of muffins that Flora handed to her. "You can start with these if you like, Ivy June," she said. "They'll be wonderful with the preserves you brought." Then she called into the kitchen, "You did an excellent job with the muffins, Flora."

Peter and Claire came next in their pajamas, just as Howard and Ezra and Danny would do back home, Ivy June thought. Mr. Combs complimented Peter for requesting the butter instead of reaching, and Claire for spreading her napkin on her lap. Catherine came to breakfast last, her hair blow-dried, wearing a thin lavender dress and shoes with a small sculptured heel. Ivy June tucked her own feet farther under her chair.

⁂

The church was a large limestone block building with curved arches over the doors. Inside, the stained-glass windows filtered the morning light over the mahogany pews, and beneath the towering gold pipes of the organ, the choir sat in their purple robes and satin stoles, waiting while the minister gave the welcome.

The congregation rose for the first hymn.

Back home in the little Buck Run Baptist Church, there were maybe a dozen hymnals; each had to serve three people at once. Ivy June hoped that the black hymnal she held now had some songs she knew—"Standing on the Promises," or "Love Lifted Me," her favorite.

This time it wasn't a hymn Ivy June knew well, but she'd heard it before, and after mouthing the words to the first verse, she sang out on the second. She especially loved the refrain:

> *Silently now I wait for Thee,*
> *Ready, my God, Thy will to see. . . .*

Mrs. Combs looked down at her and smiled, and Ivy June smiled back. But when she sang out the beautiful melody on the third verse, *"Open my heart, illumine me . . . ,"* she noticed people on both sides of her smiling her way and Ivy June wondered if she was singing too loud. Nobody worried about singing too loud in Thunder Creek. Singing was something they loved to do. And if there was one thing Ivy June was sure of, she had a good voice. Papaw could play almost any note on his guitar, and except for the highest and lowest, Ivy June could match them, pitch perfect.

Peter and Claire were in Sunday school and didn't

attend the adult service, but Ivy June enjoyed the quiet of the sanctuary and the power of the choir's anthem. She already had a dollar curled up in her hand when the offertory plate was passed, but Mr. and Mrs. Combs skipped over her and Catherine and passed the plate directly to each other. Ivy June would have put in a dollar just to have this quiet time—as close as she could get, perhaps, to the mountains.

The sermon was about giving and receiving—how the giver gets back more than he gives. When the service was over and the Combs family stood to leave, two women came over to remark on "the little songbird in our midst" and squeezed Ivy June's hand. At home in the mountains, Ivy June thought, you weren't a songbird; you just *were*. You weren't complimented on your singing; you just sang. Up here, it seemed, everything you did had to be commented on. But she could get used to that in a hurry.

◎

Flora had Sunday dinner waiting for them when they got back from church, and then she left for the day. It was something like Sunday dinner at home, Ivy June decided—the fried chicken and mashed potatoes—but at Mammaw's, there would be biscuits in place of rolls, with sausage gravy to pour over them. And there wouldn't be strawberries until they were collected wild; here they were bought frozen in a package.

Catherine's friends, Mackenzie and Hannah, came over that afternoon in shorts and T-shirts.

"I like your hair," said Hannah, whose own curly hair was pulled back straight, as though she was trying to get the curls to lie flat.

"Thank you," said Ivy June. She was glad she and Catherine had been allowed to change into jeans after church. "Anything I should know about school tomorrow?"

"The headmistress is a dragon, and the teachers are all clones," said Mackenzie.

Catherine poked her. "They are *not*! And she's already met Mrs. Fields."

"How does this program work?" Hannah asked. "You get to attend whatever classes you want?"

"I guess the Academy worked out the schedule with Thunder Creek," Ivy June told her. "I have to do all the homework, only I haven't started Spanish yet, so I can sit that one out. Go to the library or something."

"We wear uniforms," Catherine explained. "But you don't have to wear one unless you want. Mrs. Fields left one here, if you'd like to try it on."

Ivy June glanced at the others as Catherine retrieved it from her closet. "Why do you wear them?" she asked.

"So everyone will look the same," said Hannah.

"Why would you want to do that?" Ivy June was puzzled.

"We don't. We have to. It's so some girls won't try to dress better than anyone else," Mackenzie explained.

Ivy June studied the short pleated skirt. "I'll think about it," she told them.

The doorbell chimed from below, and there were sounds of running feet as Peter and Claire hurried to answer. Voices. Greetings. Catherine put one finger to her lips and Hannah and Mackenzie exchanged glances.

"Uh-oh," said Mackenzie.

"Is that who we think it is?" asked Hannah.

Catherine looked apologetically at Ivy June. "It's Dad's stepmother. Let's go down so she can't corner us up here."

Ivy June followed the others to the stairs. From the living room, she heard Mr. Combs saying, "What's Dad up to this afternoon?"

And a woman's voice answered, "If it's not golf, it's basketball. He can't wait for the NBA finals." And then the voice asked, "So how is she fitting in, Robert?" It was a low voice, somewhat impatient, as though if the speaker didn't receive a prompt reply, she'd provide the answer herself.

"She's only been here a day, Rosemary, but she seems to be fitting in fine. Went to church with us this morning," Catherine's father said.

"You won't have to drive her all the way back when she leaves, will you?" the woman's voice continued.

"It wouldn't be a problem," Mr. Combs answered.

The girls entered the living room, Ivy June trailing behind Catherine's friends.

The woman's voice said, "Hello, Mackenzie. Hi there, Hannah. Now, what have you done to those curls?" And then she saw Ivy June.

"Rosemary, this is Ivy June Mosley," said Catherine. "Ivy June, this is my grandmother."

A woman in her fifties, in a black V-necked dress, her blond hair brushed skillfully into a flip on either side of her head, extended one hand to Ivy June, who shook it cautiously. The woman's nails were long and cherry red. One leg was crossed over the other, and she wore high heels with a narrow strap across the top.

Rosemary patted the cushion beside her. "Hello, dear. Sit down and let's get acquainted." And when Ivy June obeyed, she asked, "How are you liking Lexington so far?"

"Well, I've only seen a little bit, but so far I like it fine," said Ivy June. "I'm eager to see the horses, though."

Rosemary laughed and dismissed it with a wave of her hand. "That's all anybody thinks of when they come to Lexington. Horses, horses, horses, and there's so much more to the city than that."

"Well, that's what she's here to discover," said Catherine's father. He smiled at Ivy June. "We'll keep her busy, all right!"

"But I'm so *curious*," Rosemary continued, bobbing one foot up and down. "Who really thought up this exchange program in the first place? Was it your school, Ivy June?"

"No, ma'am," Ivy June said.

"It was Buckner's idea, Grandma," said Catherine quickly.

"Grandma *Rose*mary," the woman corrected her. "Well, then how were you chosen to be the exchange student, Ivy June? I'm sure every girl in your school wanted to come."

"No, ma'am. Only six of us," said Ivy June.

Rosemary looked startled. So, actually, did the others. "Why on earth not?"

Ivy June gave a little shrug. "Afraid of the way people might treat them, maybe, I don't know."

Mrs. Combs fidgeted in her chair and reached for the glass of iced tea she'd brought into the room with her.

"And how were you selected from out of the six?" Rosemary continued.

"The principal drew my name out of a coffee can," said Ivy June.

Catherine's face was turning that funny shade of pink again, but all eyes turned to Rosemary as she said with a laugh, "Catherine had to write an essay to compete, and *you* had your name drawn out of a *coffee* can?"

"Yes, ma'am," said Ivy June, feeling the same tenseness in her jaw she'd felt when Ma and Jessie talked the way they did about Lexington. Maybe Howard was right when he said these people would just be waiting to trip her up.

Rosemary looked victoriously around the room. "Well!" she said. "I guess that goes to show!" And she focused her astonishment again on Ivy June.

"I guess so, ma'am," Ivy June said, looking straight into the woman's gray eyes. "Takes a certain kind of courage to be one of the six."

Mr. Combs burst into applause. "Bravo, Ivy June!" he said, laughing.

"We're going over to the clubhouse to play volley-ball," Catherine said hurriedly to her parents. And to Ivy June and the other girls, "Let's go, before it pours again."

Ivy June stood up as Mackenzie and Hannah edged toward the door.

"Nice to meet you, ma'am," Ivy June said to Rosemary.

And Rosemary's eyes narrowed just the slightest bit as she said, "It was nice to meet you, too."

CHAPTER TWELVE

March 9

   I expected Rosemary would be on her worst
behavior, and she "exceeded expectations," as
Dad put it. He says that she married into money
when she married Gramps and has always
been self-conscious about her own background.
That's why she's so eager to put down someone
else.

   Dad says that the way Ivy June fired back
at Rosemary shows she can stick up for herself.
And I'll have to admit I was a little bit envious
of that, because I've never had the nerve to say half
of what I feel. Our family's nothing if not polite.
We were born polite, I think, which makes me

wonder what Grandpa Combs saw in Rosemary in the first place. Or maybe, as Hannah says, Rosemary's the reason he's usually out playing golf.

We headed for the clubhouse afterward, and as soon as we got outside, Hannah said, "I'll bet you're glad that's over!" All I could do was be embarrassed. It felt good to pound that volleyball around. Ivy June must have felt it too, because she sure packed a wallop with that ball!

When I got Mom alone later, I asked what we could do about Rosemary, and she said all we could do was accept her the way she is, because "there's one in every family." Peter and Claire didn't understand the subtlety of what happened there in the living room.

"What?" they kept asking. "What did Grandma do that was so terrible?"

"She wasn't terrible," Mom explained. "She was tactless." And then it sounded to me as though she was agreeing with Rosemary but would have said it a different way. Part of me is thinking, well, if we wanted Ivy June to be just like us, why did we vote for this exchange program in the first place? And another part of me is thinking that Ivy June has a mouth on her, and underneath her politeness, there's who-knows-what waiting to make itself heard.

It's all very confusing. If something like this happens at school tomorrow, the teachers can sort it out.

Catherine Combs

CHAPTER THIRTEEN

March 10

This may be the last I write in my journal for a while, because I've got more homework than flies on a mule. What I'm wondering is, do the teachers pile on work like this every blessed day, or is it just to show me up? I gave up mud vacation for this?

We went off this morning in those short skirts— I had goose bumps clear down to my ankles. But if the other girls have to wear them, I will too. At least here you don't have to wait a half hour out on the road for a bus—Mr. Combs drives. Then Hannah's mom picks us up.

Everyone's friendly, though. There's a big

WELCOME, IVY JUNE sign above the door. Feel like I'm Miss America, almost. Then I walk inside and look like two hundred other girls, can't hardly tell them apart. I try to put names with faces, but sometimes you just have to go by knees. Seems like the knees look more different than the faces.

Catherine introduced me in every class. "This is Ivy June Mosley, our exchange student from Thunder Creek," she said. "I know that all of you will help her feel welcome." And everybody smiled at me like we've been friends since first grade.

I notice the teachers don't call on me much. That's good, because I haven't had a chance to look at a single book. Catherine said I shouldn't have to think of homework my first weekend here, but now I've got to study extra hard tonight. I have to take time to write in my journal, though, because I don't want to forget anything.

Some of the classes are harder than others. Math, for one. History's boring. I don't know if Thunder Creek's ahead of Buckner Academy or what, but we're on World War II, and they're still back with Lincoln.

English class is good, though, and I love science. They're finishing up a geology unit, and I bet it's no coincidence we're studying mountain regions of the United States, specifically the Appalachians, and in particular, the Cumberland Mountains. I knew that the Appalachians form a divide between the rivers that flow into the Atlantic Ocean and the ones that drain into the Gulf of Mexico. What I didn't know was that they're the oldest mountains in the U.S.

I walked into the science room to see a big diagram of stratified rock, like a slice cut out of a mountain. The class is studying what the earth's crust is made of, only the layers in the diagram are nice and level, like a stack of lumber. I've seen a big cut in a mountain where a road goes through, and sometimes layers are at a forty-five-degree angle. Sixty, even! Like God just leaned against a side of the mountain and the whole thing tipped over.

Everybody wants to eat with us at lunchtime, and they are so polite and sweet their words almost stick to my cheeks. I'm glad Hannah and Mackenzie eat with us, because they don't have to try so hard to be nice.

The school serves the food, and if Mammaw ever saw the stuff they put on our plates, she'd give it to a dog. Today the choice is between "mystery meat," as Catherine calls it, or grilled cheese sandwiches. I'll take a fried egg sandwich on Mammaw's homemade bread any day.

What's embarrassing, though, is that every time

I open my mouth, it's like I said something important. I mention how early I've got to get up in the morning to catch the bus in Thunder Creek, and the girls' mouths make a big O, like I just said I have to walk ten miles in the snow.

I'm writing all this from my bed. Got a bunch of pillows behind me. Catherine's over at her computer, writing an essay for English, due Friday. We've got to write two pages on someone who has influenced our life. Catherine's writing about a teacher she had last year. I thought of writing about Miss Dixon because I like her a lot, but I think I'll do Papaw instead.

Claire says I can use her computer when I need it if Catherine's using her own. I never learned the touch system of typing, though, and my handwriting is pretty good, so I may just do my essay in cursive.

I like the Combs family, all but Rosemary. She takes exception to whatever I say. I tell her I'm looking forward to seeing a horse farm, and she says, "Horses, horses, horses! That's all anybody thinks about, and Lexington is so much more than that!" She might as well have said, "Hillbillies, hillbillies, hillbillies," because I know that's what she was thinking.

Peter and Claire fuss with each other a lot, but what else is new? And I like Catherine, but I can tell we're not anywhere near being close friends yet, because she got a call on her cell phone, and when she switched it to her left ear, just before she left the room, I could hear a boy's voice. I think she's got a boyfriend, but she didn't tell me one word about him after she came back. I wonder where the girls at Buckner ever meet up with boys. Wonder too what Shirl and Fred Mason are up to during mud vacation. Got to remember to send a postcard home to Ma and Daddy so it'll get there before I get back. Catherine says we're going to do most of our sightseeing next week, when Buckner goes on spring break. I'll be glad when that happens, because I already studied the South and wouldn't want to sit through the Civil War all over again.

Ivy June Mosley

CHAPTER FOURTEEN

It seemed to Ivy June that somebody had gotten the exchange program backward. The first week should have been spring vacation—all the fun stuff—and the second week school. Then she would've had a good taste in her mouth for Lexington right off the bat.

As it was, she and Catherine were going to have to spend every evening doing homework. But right after school on Monday, they had changed out of their uniforms and gone to the clubhouse—sort of a fancy community center, Ivy June decided. This time they shot baskets, and it felt good to Ivy June.

What felt weird, though, was the way the Academy girls had come up to her that day at school, offering compliments as though they were second helpings.

"You've got beautiful teeth, Ivy June."

"I love your handwriting."

"Your back's so straight, like a ballet dancer's, almost."

"They sure must feel I need the praise," Ivy June had told Catherine at lunchtime.

"The closer we get to Friday, the more they'll forget you're here," Catherine had assured her. "I've got assignments due in every class except music, and I'll bet if Mr. Kirby could think of one to give us, he would."

She was right about that, Ivy June discovered. By Tuesday, the compliments had turned to questions—polite questions, of course: "Are there a lot of kids in your family?" and "How many grades in your school?" But by afternoon some of the girls passed Ivy June in the halls with only a smile, and Ivy June began to relax. She even began to feel less cold in the green and white pleated skirt.

Mr. Kirby's music class met twice a week, on Tuesdays and Thursdays. At Tuesday's session, he was teaching the girls a new song to be sung as a round: *Annie, Annie was the miller's daughter. Far she wandered, by the singing water. . . .* And at the end, the haunting five notes: *Bring your white sheep home.*

As the first group finished, then grew silent, Ivy June's voice stood out clear and sweet along with the second group, who repeated the concluding line: *"Bring your white sheep home."* Mr. Kirby smiled at her.

Because Buckner Academy for Girls had started out as an Episcopal school, tradition had it that each choral session end with a hymn. Every fall, during the first assembly, the school voted on the hymn of the year, Mr. Kirby explained. Last year it had been "Rock of Ages" and this year it was "Amazing Grace."

"Each week, I choose one girl to sing the third verse alone while the others hum," he said. "Would you sing it for us this time, Ivy June?"

Catherine smiled at her, but Ivy June's face flushed. Where she had sung out eagerly before, she shrank back now. "I don't remember all the words," she said.

"Here," Catherine said quickly, handing her a song sheet that the others had memorized.

Mr. Kirby smiled again and gave the pitch. The sopranos and altos hummed the first note together, then sang the rest of the verse in harmony. By the time they reached the third verse, Ivy June had regained her confidence, and sang with her eyes toward the window and the sky beyond. *Through many dangers, toils, and snares I have already come. . . .*

After all the girls joined in on the fourth verse and the song ended, Mr. Kirby smiled again and said, "Beautiful. Thank you, Ivy June."

"That was terrific!" Catherine told her later when they left the room.

"It sure was," Mackenzie agreed. "With you, it's a real song. With some of the girls, it's a competition."

"Why?" Ivy June asked.

"At the end of each year, Mr. Kirby picks the best

singer to sing it again, and he records it to play for future classes. Up to now, it's been a toss-up between Jennifer Paine and Megan Murkoff. But that was before you came along."

"Well, I'm going to leave as sudden as I came, so no use in their worrying about it," said Ivy June.

Mrs. Combs had felt good enough to make part of the dinner herself that evening, and was pleased at her progress.

"I think I just need to move around a little more to get my strength up," she said as she placed the apple cobbler on the table and let each person scoop his own ice cream. Out in the kitchen, Flora kept the TV on low as she put things away, and the rain drummed steadily on the roof and against the windows.

Peter and Claire were arguing over which of them had taken the bigger scoop and whether there was enough left for the others.

Mr. Combs grinned wearily at Ivy June. "Do your brothers argue this much?"

She smiled. "Ezra and Howard go at it sometimes, and Daddy has to take a switch to them," she said.

There were wide-eyed stares from Peter and Claire.

"He *hits* them?" asked Claire.

"He switches them a couple times on the legs and backside," said Ivy June, taking the ice cream scoop, which Claire was handing her.

Peter let a trickle of his dessert run down his chin. "He could go to jail!" he declared.

Ivy June looked amused. "Then probably every last dad in Thunder Creek would be there with him."

"Peter, in some parts of the country that's considered appropriate," said his dad.

"Danny, he's the youngest," Ivy June went on. "He's got it easier, because he sees what gets the older ones in trouble before he tries it. As Daddy says, 'Danny learns on somebody else's behind.' "

Catherine and her parents laughed while Peter and Claire tried to figure out the joke. Then Catherine said, "Probably whatever way you were raised feels right to you."

"That's a good observation, Catherine," said her dad. "I never spanked you kids because my dad never spanked me, and who knows how far back that goes?"

Ivy June tried to remember if anyone in her family had ever said to her, "That's an interesting observation." Or "Interesting thought." "Interesting argument," even. Did anyone offer praise for anything at all? Not much, she concluded. Doing or saying something intelligent was supposed to be its own reward.

There was a sudden exclamation from the kitchen.

"Oh, Lord!" came Flora's voice.

Everyone turned toward the doorway. All they could hear were the indecipherable voices on television.

"What is it, Flora?" Mrs. Combs called.

"Down near Harlan," Flora said, coming to the doorway. "Three men are trapped. . . ."

75

Ivy June jerked around, her face suddenly pale.

"Where?" she asked hoarsely. "A coal mine?"

"No, a highway crash with a tractor trailer. A trucker was injured, and a car with Illinois license plates went into the river. They've got a rescue helicopter down there now."

Peter and Claire jumped up and ran to the kitchen to watch, but Ivy June sank back in her chair, the racing in her heart beginning to slow.

Mrs. Combs shook her head. "Whenever there's rain, the roads are slick, and travelers from up north aren't used to our winding roads. . . ." She focused on Ivy June. "You were afraid it was a coal mine accident, Ivy June?"

Color returning to her cheeks, Ivy June said, "My grandfather works in a coal mine."

"No wonder you were frightened!" Mr. Combs said.

Now the whole family was watching her. Peter and Claire returned from the kitchen during a commercial.

"He's going to retire in July, though," Ivy June continued. "I sure will be glad when that happens."

"I didn't know your grandfather was a miner," said Catherine.

"Guess they left all the asking and telling up to us," Ivy June said, and wanting to deflect the attention from herself, added, "I don't know what kind of work your grandpa does either."

Mr. Combs smiled. "Well, Catherine's grandfather used to run a printing company. A very old company, actually.

Combs Printing and Engraving. My great-grandfather founded it, and now it's been handed down to me. To tell the truth, I really wanted to be a commercial pilot, but . . . it's in the family, and someday, I suppose, it will go to Peter."

"Or *me*!" said Claire.

"Of course. You or Catherine or Peter, whoever shows the most interest."

"News is back on, and they've rescued all three of them!" Flora called from the kitchen.

"Oh, that's good," said Mrs. Combs. "It's nice to have *good* news for a change."

◊◊◊

Catherine got another call from a boy that evening. Once again the girls were studying in their bedroom, away from the sounds of Claire's violin practice downstairs and Peter's video game across the hall. Ivy June saw Catherine check the number before she answered. "Hello," she said, smiling, and quickly took the phone into the bathroom, closing the door.

Ivy June was working on her essay for English, and when Catherine came out fifteen minutes later and went back to her computer, Ivy June said, "Never heard of taking a boyfriend into the bathroom with you."

Catherine turned and instantly her face colored. "He's not my boyfriend," she said, then sat down quickly and worked the keyboard.

For ten seconds or so, the room was quiet except for the soft sound of keys clicking. Then Catherine stole a look at Ivy June. Ivy June was still watching her, and suddenly both girls broke into laughter.

"Not my *boy*friend!" Catherine insisted.

"No skin off my nose. *I* don't like him!" said Ivy June.

"He's just a guy I met at a party last Christmas," Catherine explained. "A friend of a friend, that's all."

"Fine with me," said Ivy June, grinning.

"But don't tell anyone," said Catherine.

"Not a word," Ivy June promised.

CHAPTER FIFTEEN

March 11

There's something I need to write about. On the news tonight, there was a report of three men trapped in a sinking car down near Harlan, and a helicopter rescue. At first, Ivy June was afraid it was a coal mine accident, and we found out that her grandfather works in a mine. There's so much I don't know about Ivy June.

Afterward, we were doing homework in my room, kidding around . . . talking. . . . But later, when I came out of the bathroom, I saw her slip something under her pillow. I could tell by the way she did it that it was something she didn't want me to see. I didn't want to say anything, but I began to suspect she'd stolen something of mine.

I hated myself for suspecting it, but still, I couldn't let it go. I was afraid it was the gold locket from Mom, or maybe the ring from Rosemary and Gramps. When Ivy June went in the bathroom next and I heard the bathwater running, I knew that if I didn't find out what she'd hidden, I'd go on suspecting everything she did for the rest of her time here. And if she _was_ stealing . . . well, better to have it out now.

I peeked under her pillow, and there was a small rock. Just a rock. I could feel my face redden because I was so wrong, and I put the pillow back. Then, hearing Ivy June splashing around in the tub, I lifted the pillow again and picked up the rock. It was rough on one side, smooth on the other. Nothing more unusual about it. I can't understand. And there's no way I can ask Ivy June about it without admitting I peeked.

Catherine Combs

CHAPTER SIXTEEN

A Person Who Influenced My Life
by Ivy June Mosley

His name is Spencer Mosley, but he's Papaw to
me. He's my grandfather, on Daddy's side, and
he's sixty-four years old. I live with him and
Mammaw now, because our own house got too
small for the seven of us, and Papaw asked could I
live with them. Ma says that after children get
shoulder high, they just take up more space, and
we only have two bedrooms.

Papaw Mosley is a miner. There aren't that many
deep mines left where we live, but Papaw's one of
those miners. If you lined him up with the other

men, he wouldn't stand out particularly except he'd be older than most, which is why he's retiring this summer.

He's got ears that stick way out the sides of his head, and a large enough nose to suit his face. His eyebrows have turned gray like his hair, and there's not much left of that, but he's got a strong chin. It's his eyes I like, though, because they're always smiling, even when his mouth isn't. The little crinkles in the skin at the corners fan out when he smiles, like his lips and his eyes are connected by the same string. He's got the biggest hands and feet of any man I ever saw.

What I learned from Papaw is that every single thing you can learn to do makes you feel that much better about yourself, even something as small as frying an egg.

Papaw stays busy, whether he's at the mine or not. He used to take Howard and me out in the woods to dig roots—bloodroot and ginseng. Taught us how to dry it so we could sell it when we got a pound. Taught us how to plant corn and beans on the new moon, and to catch crawdads in Thunder Creek.

Here are some more things I've learned to do: skin a squirrel if I have to, shoot a rifle, build a fence, sew a quilt, tell starroot from stoneroot, make corn bread, feed Grandmommy, wash clothes, cut hair, change babies, and name the books of the Bible. If I was to find myself alone in the mountains for a year, I could take care of myself.

"Learn to do for yourself, because that's all you can really depend on," Papaw says.

I wonder sometimes what Papaw thinks about when he's in the mine. If it wasn't that he's helping support my family back at the house, he and Mammaw would have an inside toilet and maybe even a bathtub by now. "We don't have much, but we're rich as the Lord wants us to be," he says.

Papaw also says the secret to life is wanting what you have. The thing is, when you grow up without knowing what you don't have, you don't miss it. Once you know about it, though, you keep remembering. I do want what I have, but if you don't reach for something more—I don't mean things, I mean more from yourself—how can you grow? And you won't ever reach for it if you don't start wanting it in the first place.

Papaw is the person who has influenced me most, because he sees in me what I can't even see myself. He knows what I can do before I learn to do it. I guess that gives me confidence—enough to come to Lexington and see how other people live. And he'll be the first one I tell about it when I get back.

CHAPTER SEVENTEEN

There was one two-hour art class each week at Buckner, and it met on Wednesdays. Ivy June had been secretly looking forward to this class, eager to have someone outside of Thunder Creek recognize her talent. When she followed Catherine into the studio, however, and looked at the sketches and paintings there on the walls, she felt she must have walked into an art gallery.

There were drawings of faces so real that they looked like black-and-white photographs. Paintings of flowers so feathery that she didn't quite see how a brush could make such a mark on canvas. There were still lifes of apples and pears, each done in a different artistic style, so that while you were looking at the same plate with the knife and the fruit and the cheese, you could tell that each artist saw a different image in her mind.

Miss Lorenzo greeted Ivy June warmly and asked the girls to arrange themselves in a circle around a small raised platform. When the desks had been noisily rearranged, she asked if one of the girls would volunteer to be their model.

"Do I have to take off my clothes?" Mackenzie quipped, and everyone laughed, including the teacher.

"No, I'd just like you to sit in a relaxed position—one arm thrown over the back of the chair, maybe," the teacher said. "Try that, see if it's comfortable. See if you can hold it for an hour and a half."

While Mackenzie tried out different positions on the platform, Miss Lorenzo talked about how each student would be drawing the model from a different angle. The same girl, in the same chair, but each artist would see her from a different perspective.

As the teacher moved about the room, commenting on the strokes, the shading, Ivy June knew that she probably had one of the easiest angles. She was drawing Mackenzie from the side, and it was a lot easier drawing the profile of a forehead, nose, and chin than it was to draw the face full front and get the shading just right.

"Excellent!" Miss Lorenzo said to some. "Great foreshortening there, Maria," or, "Take another look at her left hand, Courtney. Check the proportions."

When she came to Ivy June's sketch, she studied it a moment, then said, "Your details are good, but look at the figure as a whole—the relaxed slump of the shoulder, for example. You'll want to see the shape of the whole in your mind before you concentrate on details, but keep working."

Ivy June stared hard at her sketch. The teacher was right. The whole pose was wrong on paper. In her drawing, the girl's posture was stiff, unnatural, but she had great pleats in her skirt.

At the end of the period, when all the sketches were collected and propped along the chalk tray beneath the blackboard, Ivy June realized that while a few of the other drawings were as amateurish as her own, most were far more artistic, more natural, more original. Miss Lorenzo pointed out the features of the best work, and it was what she didn't say about the others that said it all.

She was subdued over the lunch hour, and was glad for free time in the library later, when she could write home on the stamped postcards Mammaw had given her.

Dear Ma and Daddy (and Jessie, Howard, Ezra, and Danny),

I'm going to drop this myself in a mailbox I saw at the corner because I don't want anyone to read it but you. I'm here, no car wreck or anything, and I have a bed to myself in the Combses' big house. They're nice people for the most part and we went to church on Sunday. The choir sang fine, but nobody opens their mouth very wide. Peter and Claire, the ten-year-old twins, are pretty funny

86

sometimes. School is hard in some classes, easy in others. Hope the creek didn't rise too much.

Love, Ivy June

Dear Papaw, Mammaw, and Grandmommy:

I'm here without a car wreck, but I miss you a lot. Mrs. Combs thanks you for the preserves and says blackberry's her favorite. She has someone do the cooking for her because she's been sick, but it's nothing as good as yours. I've got a bed to myself and it's a right big house here. Everybody's nice to me except Catherine's step-grandmother, Rosemary, but Catherine doesn't like her either. I'll mail this postcard myself so no one else will see it. Hope the creek didn't rise too much.

Love and kisses, Ivy June

Despite her disappointment about the art class, Ivy June fell into the rhythm of the school day and the Combs household. Taking turns in the bathroom each morning with Catherine and Claire, riding to school with Catherine's dad, or sometimes Mackenzie's. Classes till three, then the ride home again—a snack in the kitchen, shooting baskets over at the clubhouse with Catherine, then dinner, and homework till almost nine. Ivy June treated herself to a bath each night, luxuriating in the hot water.

At Buckner she was in the general math class, not the

advanced. The teacher was talking about interest rates. If the list price of a new car was $20,000, she said, and the dealer gave you eight years to pay it off at $350 a month, what was the rate of interest? How much would you actually end up paying for the car? The girls busied themselves with calculations at their desks and gasped as one by one they discovered that they would be paying $33,600 for a $20,000 car.

Ivy June tried to remember if anyone she had ever known had bought a new car at any price. Most of the cars that belonged to people in Thunder Creek had been sold and resold, so that by the time it got to you, you were maybe the third or fourth owner.

The last class of the day was science, with its unit on geology. Mrs. Baker was talking about the age of rocks—about carbon dating and how it helps tell how old a fossil is.

"Think about this, girls," she said. "Some people dismiss geology as nothing more than the study of silent, unmoving rock. . . . What's wrong with that statement?"

"Rock does move over centuries," answered one girl.

"And when volcanoes erupt, you can hear it," said Hannah.

Ivy June slowly raised her hand. "But there doesn't even have to be an eruption to hear a mountain," she said. "My grandfather works in a coal mine, and he said that when you're deep down, you can hear the mountain groan and shift."

There was complete silence in the room.

"Tell us about it, Ivy June," the teacher said.

Ivy June worked hard to get it right. "There was this day that Papaw was working a tunnel and the roof caved in," she continued. And in the minutes that followed, she found herself telling how the miners had been trapped by a huge slab of slate. How they'd listened that whole night for rescuers, but all they could hear were the sounds of rock itself. "Like a handful of marbles rubbing together," Ivy June finished, remembering the way Papaw had described it another time.

No one moved.

"That's something we wouldn't have known if you hadn't been here to tell us," Mrs. Baker said.

"How was your grandfather rescued?" one girl asked.

And Ivy June told how the team had kept drilling from the other side of the rock fall until finally they could break through and reach the miners.

"Imagine it," the teacher said, "working six hundred feet below the surface, surrounded by rock that had been changed from ancient flowers and ferns to peat. The pressure of the water above squeezed it down until it formed coal."

On the board she wrote, *Five to eight feet of rotted plants = one foot of coal.*

"If you look closely at a piece of coal," she went on, "you may be able to see the markings of plants and ferns. In some mines the workers have no light except that provided by their helmet lamps. No air except that which is pumped through their ventilation system. I want you to think about this over spring break, about all the ways coal makes our lives better. Think of the risks that miners take to get it for us."

∭

On Thursday in Mr. Kirby's music class, the girls sang the Annie song again, and now that they knew the words and the melody, it was all the more beautiful. But Ivy June was astounded, as the period was ending, to hear Mr. Kirby say, "Ivy June, it's been a real pleasure having you in this class, and I think I've found the voice I'd like to record for our hymn of the year. I hope the rest of you will agree with my choice. Would you sing the third verse again of 'Amazing Grace,' and this time I'll record it?"

There was polite applause from some of the other girls, but not, Ivy June noticed, from either Jennifer Paine or Megan Murkoff.

"Um . . . ," Ivy June said, embarrassed.

"You're our first exchange student, and you'd be doing us an honor by being our guest singer."

"Okay," Ivy June said, and her face felt warm.

She tried not to look at Jennifer or Megan when she sang the solo, but her voice was thin this time, and didn't carry the expression she had felt the first time she had sung it.

"Let's do it again," Mr. Kirby said. "Take some deep breaths, Ivy June, and really let it out when it's your time to sing."

Catherine seemed to know what the problem was. At

any rate, she leaned over Ivy June's shoulder and whispered, "Let's hear it for Thunder Creek!"

Ivy June remembered that she was the ambassador. Whatever she did or didn't do would reflect on Miss Dixon and the people back home. She fixed her eyes once more on the sky beyond the window, and when it was her time to sing, she let it out, just as Mr. Kirby had said.

"Wonderful," he told her as he played it back and they all listened. "That's a wonderful gift, Ivy June."

CHAPTER EIGHTEEN

It was only seven days ago in Thunder Creek that Ivy June had celebrated the last day before vacation, and now she was doing it again here with Catherine. Spring break at Buckner came the week before Easter, and teachers didn't give assignments to be done over that period. The sun was out for the first time since her arrival, and Ivy June looked forward to doing something fun.

At the start of school on Friday, Jennifer Paine stopped by Catherine's locker.

"Hey, are you guys going to be around tonight? Thought I'd have a sleepover in honor of Ivy June before everyone takes off for vacation."

"Oh!" Catherine looked at Ivy June uncertainly. "Sounds fun. I'll have to call Mom and see if she's got anything planned. I'll let you know."

"Tacos at seven!" Jennifer said, and made her way through the throng of girls to another locker.

Catherine hung up her jacket and turned to Ivy June. "I didn't know what to say. I wasn't sure if you'd want to go."

Ivy June wasn't sure either. She'd only been on an overnight once, and had shared the room with Shirl and her two sisters. She'd known what to expect there, however, and had no idea what it would be like at Jennifer's.

"What about you? Do you want to go?" Ivy June asked. "She's a friend, right?"

"Not a close one," said Catherine. "Tell you what. If she's invited Hannah and Mackenzie, we'll go. If not, I'll make an excuse."

◯◯◯

It seemed strange to turn in work she would never see again, in classes she would never come back to, Ivy June thought as they went from class to class that morning. She was glad, actually, that she would never have to see what grade she got on her math paper, though she knew she'd done well on the quiz about the Civil War.

At lunchtime, Catherine called her mom on her cell phone and found there was nothing special planned for that evening. And because Mackenzie and Hannah were also going to the sleepover, she told Jennifer that she and Ivy June could come.

The halls were filled with excited chatter about the

coming week, with lots of goodbyes, as though the girls were parting for good. A few even hugged Ivy June. Back home, all she had said to Shirl that last day was "Have a good time with Fred Mason."

As Catherine, Ivy June, Mackenzie, and Hannah waited for Hannah's mom to pick them up that afternoon, Catherine said, "We'll see you guys at Jennifer's tonight. We probably wouldn't be going if you weren't. You can never tell about Jennifer."

"Our family's flying to Washington tomorrow afternoon," Hannah said. "We'll be spending the week visiting the Capitol and stuff."

"We're just going to Cincinnati for a couple of days," said Mackenzie.

Ivy June listened in amazement. People talked of driving to Cincinnati or flying to Washington as easily as Daddy might talk about driving to Hazard—did anyone want to come along? And even that didn't happen very often.

Hannah's mom pulled into the school driveway, and the girls edged toward the curb.

"What did you mean, Catherine, that with Jennifer you never can tell?" Ivy June asked, still puzzled about the sleepover.

Catherine and Mackenzie exchanged looks.

"Just that . . . Jennifer . . . well, Jennifer's Jennifer," Catherine said, not very helpfully.

"She's fine as long as she's the star of the show,"

Mackenzie explained. "But don't worry. The sleepover's at her house, so she'll be the star of the show."

〽️

Jennifer's house was half again as big as Catherine's, with tall white columns on the porch and an entrance hall two stories high.

A sleek blond woman in great jeans and a blue shirt greeted the girls when they stepped inside.

"I'm Jennifer's mom," the woman said, extending her hand to Ivy June. "I hope you're enjoying your stay in Lexington."

"Yes, ma'am," said Ivy June.

"And how's your mother, Catherine?" Mrs. Paine asked.

"A little stronger, I think," Catherine answered just as the doorbell rang again and Jennifer came skittering down the curving staircase to pull her guests inside.

All the girls dropped their bags in the large family room at the back of the house, then trooped into the kitchen, where Mrs. Paine had left all the taco ingredients on the counter. Guests helped themselves to the meat mixture and toppings, then sat down on the couches and floor of the family room to eat. Ivy June looked about her. This space was probably as big as all the rooms in Mammaw's house put together. A huge stone fireplace covered the wall at one end; a grand piano sat at the other end. The bank of windows along one wall stretched from floor to ceiling.

"So tell us about Thunder Creek, Ivy June," Megan Murkoff said. "What do you do for fun? Do you have sleepovers like this?"

"Not very often," Ivy June answered. "Our houses are pretty far apart, and there's not always someone around to drive us."

"Do you have best friends?"

"Shirl's my best. 'Best pest,' I call her," Ivy June said, and the girls laughed. "She's a cutup."

"Where do you go when you go out?" asked Courtney.

"Sometimes we go down to Earl Parker's store on Friday or Saturday nights. Anyone with a fiddle is welcome to stop by and play. Or Earl puts on a CD and plays it over a loudspeaker, and we dance out in the parking lot."

"So you have electricity?" asked Jennifer.

"Yeah, and most houses have telephones, but we don't. Phone company keeps promising to string a line, but there's only a few of us at the south end of the hollow, so they're not rushing themselves."

"Cell phone?" asked Catherine.

"Not in the hollows. The town of Thunder Creek is in a service area, but we're not."

"Then what do you do in an emergency?" Hannah asked. "What if someone was trying to reach you?"

"They'd probably try the school first, or Earl's, if it was night. Then somebody would drive up and deliver the news. Or sometimes they'll reach us through Sam Feeley and his ham radio. He lives back up the mountain a ways, not too far. He'll get on his horse and ride over," Ivy June told them.

"Like something out of a storybook!" Megan exclaimed.

Ivy June smiled. "No storybook, exactly."

The conversation turned to school again, and after the taco crumbs were cleared away and Megan passed around the brownies she had brought, Jennifer told Ivy June they were going to give her the official "Buckner welcome"—trim her hair, do her fingernails, and polish her toenails.

Ivy June glanced at Catherine, but Catherine seemed to be saying this was okay. So, somewhat embarrassed, Ivy June pulled off her shoes, wondering when she'd last cut that toenail on her left foot that was digging a hole in her sock. But since the rest of the girls were tending to each other, she decided to be a good sport.

Someone put on a CD, and as the nail polish and emery boards were brought out, Courtney put a towel around Ivy June's shoulders and produced a pair of scissors.

"I don't want it any shorter," Ivy June said.

"I'm just going to even up the back, that's all," said Courtney, and Ivy June could feel the side of the scissors traveling slowly in a horizontal line beneath her shoulder blades. Jennifer, on her left, polished her left toenails and fingernails; a girl on her right did the other foot and hand.

"Feel like I'm a queen or something," Ivy June said, and the girls looked up from their polishing and smiled.

When nails were dry and Megan was passing around her brownies again, Jennifer turned off the CD and moseyed to the piano. She sat down and idly began picking out a tune, then settled into a beautiful piece, playing more deliberately. She obviously had it memorized.

"What's this, Ivy June?" she called as she played.

"I don't know, but it's pretty," Ivy June said, blowing on the nails of one hand.

"You don't know it?" said Megan, seeming surprised.

Jennifer stopped and began playing something else. "Well, what's this one, then?" she asked.

It was vaguely familiar, but Ivy June didn't know it either. She shook her head.

"It's only by one of the greatest composers for piano in the whole world," said Jennifer.

Ivy June saw Mackenzie and Hannah exchange glances.

"Chopin!" said Megan, an exaggerated expression of disbelief on her face.

Jennifer stopped playing a second time, and began still a third number. "You've *got* to know this," she said, frowning a little at Ivy June.

"The Moonlight Sonata," said Ivy June, in a soft, embarrassed voice.

"Riiiiiight! And the composer?" said Megan.

"Hey, I thought school was over for the week!" said Catherine quickly.

"Yeah, let's watch the movie," said Mackenzie.

A DVD was produced, and Jennifer got up from the piano. Courtney brushed the hair clippings off Ivy June's shirt and said, "You know, we're about the same size. I've got a great-looking shirt I don't wear anymore, if you want it."

Another girl turned around. "What size shoe do you wear, Ivy June? I wear a seven, and I've got some sandals I'll bet you'd like."

"Thanks, but I don't have any more room in my suitcase," Ivy June told them, and headed for the bathroom to brush off the hair around her neck.

She closed the door, her cheeks bright pink, and stared at her reflection in the mirror. Courtney had done a good job with her hair, but how much of what had gone on out there was well intended? The music quiz seemed designed to prove that she hadn't deserved to be the school's soloist.

Ivy June took a deep breath and held it. She wanted to leave. Wished she were back at Shirl's, teasing her about Fred Mason, horsing around with Shirl's sisters, reading their magazines. But Miss Dixon had called her the ambassador from their school, so ambassador she was going to be. Ivy June exhaled, brushed the hair off her shoulders, and went back out to the family room.

When it came time to sleep, the girls unrolled sleeping bags or settled down on one of the three couches. Ivy June finally fell asleep, only to be wakened about seven in the morning when Jennifer's eight-year-old brother sneaked into the room and began playing "Chopsticks" on the piano.

〰

There were Belgian waffles for breakfast, with whipped cream and strawberries, and the girls sat around in their pajamas, hair uncombed, looking and acting more like fifth than seventh graders. They teased each other, Ivy June included, spotting each other's cheeks with fingers dipped in strawberry juice, until they all looked as though they had the measles.

Ivy June loved being included in the fun. Now that Jennifer and Megan had shown her up with their musical knowledge, it seemed she had passed the friendship test. Everyone was laughingly dumping their whipped cream on top of Jennifer's waffle, just because Jennifer loved whipped cream so much. Ivy June put her scoop on last, so it towered over the others; then she picked up a slice of strawberry and delicately set it on top, where it balanced on one end. Everyone cheered.

There was talk of what each girl would be doing during spring break—who was traveling, who would be in town, and who the contact person would be if someone decided to give a party.

"Cat will be here all week; she'll let us know," Megan said.

"Ha," Catherine joked, leaning her head sleepily on one hand. "Nobody ever calls me."

"Except her boyfriend," said Ivy June, grinning. Then her heart jumped to her throat as Catherine jerked upright. The girls all hooted, curious.

"I don't have a boyfriend," Catherine said, staring hard at Ivy June, her eyes cold.

The rest of the girls began to laugh.

"Aha!" said Jennifer. "Do I detect a rise in temperature?"

"So who is he?" asked Hannah.

"I was just kidding," Ivy June said quickly. "How would I know?" But no one believed her.

"I *said* I don't have a boyfriend!" Catherine repeated, and stabbed at another bite of waffle.

All the girls were smiling now—all but Mackenzie.

"How many times has he called, Ivy June?" one of the girls asked.

"She doesn't have a boyfriend," said Ivy June. "I was just shooting off my mouth."

"So do *you* have a boyfriend back home?" Courtney asked her.

"Sure. Dozens," said Ivy June. "Got 'em lined up all the way to Tennessee."

The girls laughed again, all but Catherine and Mackenzie.

Later, as the girls dressed and collected their things, Ivy June could barely look at Catherine. How could she have *said* that? Hadn't she promised not to mention the boy's calls to anyone? How could she stay another week at the Combses' with Catherine mad at her? Sleeping in the same room?

She stuffed her things into the overnight bag Claire had loaned her and pulled on her jacket. When Ivy June went out on the porch to wait for Mr. Combs to pick them up, Catherine turned away. And when the car pulled into the driveway, Catherine got in first without saying a word.

CHAPTER NINETEEN

When the girls got home, Catherine went inside and ran directly up the stairs to her room. Miserably, Ivy June followed. She was afraid, when Catherine shut the door behind her, that she might have locked it. But no, the door opened. Ivy June watched Catherine drop her overnight bag on the floor, plunk herself down on the bed, and turn her face to the wall.

Ivy June sat down on the edge of the other bed. She started to speak once, but her voice only produced a squeak. She tried again: "Catherine, I'm really sorry."

There was no response.

"I don't know what made me say that. It came out so fast."

Still nothing from Catherine, except a slight shrug of a shoulder, as though nothing Ivy June could say would make it better.

"As soon as I said it, I knew I shouldn't have," Ivy June told her pleadingly.

Catherine jerked around. "You *promised* you wouldn't say a word!"

"I know. And I feel awful."

"Not as awful as *I* feel," Catherine said, with anger.

There was silence in the bedroom for a few moments.

"Like I said, I'm really, really sorry, but . . . Well, what's wrong with having a boyfriend? I mean, if he *is* your boyfriend!"

"I *told* you he's not!" Catherine shot back. "And now Mackenzie's mad at me, and she's like my best friend in the whole world. *Was*, I should say!"

"But why should she be mad?" Ivy June asked.

Catherine sat up completely and swung her legs over the side of the bed, glaring at Ivy June. "Because she likes him too, and she didn't know he's been calling me, that's why."

"Oh," said Ivy June, trying to figure it out. "Then he's Mackenzie's boyfriend?"

"He's *no*body's boyfriend!" Catherine said. "And it's none of your business."

"Okay. I'm sorry." Ivy June pulled her legs up on the bed and wrapped her arms around her knees. She and Catherine were quiet for a while. Once, the girls lifted their eyes and glanced at each other, then dropped them again.

Finally Catherine sighed and scooted back against the wall. "Look. Every February our school puts on a carnival along with St. John's to raise money for our libraries. St. John's is a boys' school. This year we met Andy at one of the booths, and he was really cute. *That's* who he is."

Ivy June nodded, and Catherine continued: "Mackenzie hung around him all evening and flirted a lot. I did too, actually. For the last three weeks, all she's talked about is Andy. And when he started calling me . . . well, how could I tell her?"

"I don't know. I guess you couldn't," said Ivy June. "But how would she know it's him who's been calling?"

"Who else would it be?" said Catherine. "Mackenzie and Hannah and I tell each other everything. Well, *almost* everything. If there was any boy other than Andy calling me, I would have told her already, and she knows it."

They sat across from each other on the twin beds, studying each other's feet. Finally Ivy June said, "What can I do to make up for it?"

"If I knew, I'd tell you. I don't think there's anything you can say to Mackenzie now to keep her from being mad at me."

"Don't you think she already suspected that he likes you?" Ivy June asked cautiously. "I mean, girls can tell about things like this."

"I don't know, but you sure ruined things between us," Catherine said.

Ivy June rested her chin on her arms. When she looked up again, she said, "Are you going to be mad at me the whole rest of the time I'm here?"

Catherine didn't answer for a moment. She might

have been holding back a smile; Ivy June wasn't sure. "Probably," Catherine said.

"Well, is there anything I can do to make you *not* be mad at me?"

Catherine thought it over. "Yes. Tell me one of *your* secrets."

"For you to tell the other girls?"

"Maybe. If I feel like it."

Ivy June took a deep breath. "Okay," she said. "I kissed a boy once at Shirl's."

Catherine did smile a little bit. "Shirl's your best friend?"

"Yeah. We started first grade together."

"Who was the boy?"

"Jimmy Harris. We were playing spin the bottle and I had to kiss him in front of everybody."

"Then that's not a secret," said Catherine. "That doesn't count."

Ivy June thought some more. "Okay, then. I stole something once from Walmart."

"Really? What was it?"

"Uh . . . a pair of socks."

"You did not," said Catherine.

"How do you know?"

"I just know. If you'd stolen anything, it wouldn't be socks, and I'll bet you never stole anything in your life."

Ivy June sighed. "Okay, I didn't."

"If I'm not going to be mad at you for the next week,

106

you've got to tell me something that's really, *really* secret,"
said Catherine.

"All right, but I'll have to think about it," said Ivy June.

For the time being, the secret was put on hold because
Mrs. Combs had tickets that evening to *Oklahoma!* at the
Lexington Opera House, and they would all be going out
to dinner before the performance.

"Yes, you have to wear a tie. Quit fussing about it," Ivy
June heard Mr. Combs say to Peter, who was complaining
loudly. "We *always* wear ties to the theater, and you know
that."

To Catherine, Ivy June said, "I guess I'm supposed to
dress up as much as I possibly can?"

"Next to weddings and funerals," Catherine told her.

Ivy June put on the same dress and sandals she'd worn
to church but accepted the offer of Catherine's light wool
jacket instead of the grimy one she'd worn with her jeans
when she'd arrived.

As Ivy June was brushing her hair at the mirror in the
bathroom, the knob turned on the other door and Claire
stepped in.

"Oh!" she said. "It wasn't locked."

"It's okay. I'm about to leave," Ivy June told her.

"How do I look?" Claire stood perfectly still, her chin
held high for inspection.

"I think you look terrific," Ivy June said, noting the
black velvet top and taffeta skirt. Then she leaned down a

107

little closer. "Hmmm. Either strawberry jam or your ma's lip gloss, I'll bet."

Claire quickly backed away, but her eyes danced. "Only a little," she said. "Catherine uses it sometimes. I saw!"

"Well then, that's Catherine's secret, isn't it?"

The young girl leaned against the doorframe and watched as Ivy June gathered up her comb and brush and the talcum powder Mammaw had given her to pat under her arms. "Is it true that everyone in Thunder Creek is poor?" Claire asked, and then, suddenly conscious of her rudeness, said, "Not you, I mean."

"Well, I don't know of any rich people," Ivy June said, and couldn't help admiring Claire's frankness.

But Claire was stumbling all over herself now to make amends. "I've heard it's really beautiful in the mountains, and there's no traffic or anything."

"You're right," said Ivy June, leaving the bathroom. "It doesn't have a lot of things, and tons of cars are one of them."

She knew, of course. They had all known why Buckner Academy had chosen Thunder Creek, in one of the poorest counties in Kentucky. She knew she was coming to Lexington as a disadvantaged girl, to get a taste of the finer things in life—by city standards, of course. But so what? She was here, she was hungry to learn, and she was going to enjoy everything the night had to offer.

⚭

Catherine, too, looked nice that evening. She wasn't an exceptionally pretty girl, but she was attractive when she was all dressed up. She wore the same gold locket with everything, jeans and dresses alike. On this night it shone against her dress of green silk. It was her mother's locket. She had worn it as a girl, Catherine had explained to Ivy June, opening it to show a tiny photo of her mother at age fifteen.

"Mom used to carry a photo of *her* mom inside it," she said.

"Well!" said Catherine's father, looking about the big round table at the restaurant once they were seated. "It's great to have us all together and in a good mood."

He had sensed the quarrel between her and Catherine that afternoon, Ivy June was certain, and this was his way of saying he was glad it was over.

Mrs. Combs opened the menu. "We're celebrating two things tonight—the start of spring break, and having Ivy June as our guest," she said. "So I hope you will order whatever you like, Ivy June."

"Us too?" asked Claire.

"Of course," said their mother. "As long as you eat something besides French fries."

There were things on the menu Ivy June had never heard of, and it seemed to take a long time after they had ordered for the food to arrive. Ivy June was thinking that back in Hazard or Harlan, they could have eaten three or four meals at McDonald's in the time it took to eat one dinner at a restaurant in Lexington. Nevertheless, she enjoyed her chicken pot pie while the others ate veal, and was surprised to see bread pudding, a favorite of Mammaw's, on the menu for dessert.

Her legs got cold on the walk from the restaurant to the opera house. Catherine, she noticed, was wearing panty hose, which Ivy June had never worn in her life. But once inside the beautiful theater, Ivy June stood gazing up at the ceiling, which was so high she couldn't imagine how anyone could have put lights there. The red plush seats, the two curved balconies with their fancy boxes at either end—she'd have to remember to write it all down later in her journal.

If Jessie could see me now, she thought, almost guiltily, and wished that Howard and Ezra and Danny could see it too. Wished that Ma and Daddy had the time and the money to come to a place like this. That Mammaw and Papaw could sit in a restaurant and be served by waiters in blue jackets. And that Shirl could sit beside her in the theater and giggle at the man in front of them, who was wearing a collar so tight it looked as though he were choking. Then the orchestra started to play. The curtain rose on a prairie scene, and a man sitting on a fence began singing, *"Oh, what a beautiful mornin'. . . ."* Ivy June was hooked.

During intermission, when everyone stood at once and began surging up the aisle to the exits, Ivy June felt her throat tighten and perspiration bead up on her forehead. The crush of people! This was far worse than the halls at school. No one seemed to be moving much at all, just inching forward bit by bit. She could feel their breath on the back of her neck, their feet bumping into her heels,

110

but there was no place to go. She kept bumping into people herself as she was propelled forward, saying "Excuse me" and "Pardon me" and "Oops!" and "I'm sorry."

As soon as they reached the lobby, Ivy June made her way to a clear space just inside the entrance and stood taking deep breaths.

"You okay?" Catherine asked, coming up beside her.

"Yeah," Ivy June answered, her voice a little shaky.

"Want a Sprite or anything?"

"No, I'm fine," Ivy June said, but when they got back to their seats and she checked the program again, she was glad to see that there were no more intermissions.

◊◊◊

"Did you like it?" Claire asked when they were out on the sidewalk again, heading back to the parking lot.

"I loved it!" Ivy June said. "I knew some of those songs already. We sang them at school."

"Well, we have a lot of things planned for you, Ivy June," Mrs. Combs told her. "I hope we won't wear you out." Claire was hugging her mom's side before Peter eased himself between them to claim their mother for himself. Claire elbowed him furiously, and Mrs. Combs had to separate the twins, one on either side of her.

"Ivy June thought she was going to be trampled to death at intermission," Catherine joked.

Mr. Combs looked down at Ivy June. "Not used to crowds, huh?"

"Papaw says every man should live far enough away from his neighbors that he can't see their chimney smoke, but close enough so he could hear them yell," Ivy June explained.

Everyone laughed.

"Do you think he'd like Lexington?" asked Peter.

"Maybe for a while, but he says he can't imagine living in a place where he can't see hills," Ivy June said. "You look out a window in Thunder Creek, you won't see anything *but* hills."

She was glad to get in the car again, and pulled the hem of her dress down over her knees for warmth. She was glad too that Catherine was friendly toward her again—was talking to her, anyway—and hoped that as the days went on, Catherine would forget about making her tell a secret.

But just after the light was out that night, before the girls fell asleep, she heard Catherine say, "Remember, Ivy June. Your most *secret* secret!"

"Okay," Ivy June said. "But you'll have to wait till my last day. I'll tell you then."

"Why do I have to wait?" asked Catherine. "Is it that awful?"

"Worse," said Ivy June.

CHAPTER TWENTY

March 15

   I guess if I never saw any more of Lexington than the opera house, I'd say I've seen a lot. I've seen a whole bunch of seats before, like at graduation in our gym, but not a thousand, and none of them in red velvet you could sink down three inches in. The chicken pie was good too, but they don't know how to make biscuits like Mammaw does.
   I've got to come up with a secret, though, and Catherine's not going to listen to any spin the bottle stories, either. I hope we're still friends when Mackenzie gets back from Cincinnati.

                                        Ivy June Mosley

March 15

I was so mad at Ivy June this morning I didn't even want to say her name. I couldn't believe she said what she did at Jennifer's, and Mackenzie knew, I could tell. Maybe Ivy June's right—maybe Mackenzie has suspected all along that Andy likes me, but Ivy June sort of made it official. Can I help it if a boy likes me, though? What am I supposed to do—hang up on him?

It's hard to stay mad at Ivy June for long, because she's so direct about everything, but I'm not going to let her off easy. She's going back to Thunder Creek with a secret of mine, and I'm going to make sure she leaves one of hers behind.

Catherine Combs

CHAPTER TWENTY-ONE

After church on Sunday, the family had barely finished
their noon meal when Rosemary arrived.

"John," she said to Catherine's father, "your dad is
away at a golf tournament this weekend, and I have a
wonderful idea. I'm going to take Ivy June shopping, and
Catherine can come along if she likes."

Ivy June had just taken a sip of iced tea, and started to
speak as she swallowed. She coughed instead.

"Shopping?" asked Mrs. Combs.

"I . . . I don't need anything," Ivy June said.

"I didn't say you *needed* anything, dear. But I'm afraid
I came across as rude last week, and I want to make
amends. I *want* to take you shopping and send you back
home with a brand-new outfit, head to toe."

How do you politely say no to a woman who maybe is

trying to be nice? Ivy June wondered. She didn't want to show up in Thunder Creek with a brand-new outfit. Did not want to go to school with new shoes. Did not want anything about her to look as though she had changed. The last thing in the world she wanted was to come back from Lexington looking like she was trying to be better than anyone else.

"No, thank you," she said.

Rosemary looked at her in astonishment. "Dear, I'm not expecting you to pay for it! This is a gift from me to you, and Catherine can come along to help pick things out."

"Yes, ma'am, I appreciate it. But I . . . I really just don't want to," Ivy June said haltingly.

"That's fair, Ivy June," Mr. Combs said firmly. "Rosemary, why don't you sit down and have some dessert with us? Ivy June had quite a day yesterday, and I imagine she'd just like to rest."

Rosemary was still staring at her.

"Well, I can hardly see how she could refuse a new outfit," she said. "If anyone had offered that to me when *I* was her age, I would have thought I'd died and gone to heaven."

"If you'd died and gone to heaven, you wouldn't *need* new clothes," said Peter, and everyone laughed. Everyone but Rosemary.

She sat down stiffly in a chair next to Claire. "One of the things I learned as a girl was to be grateful," she said.

116

"When I saw a chance to better myself, I took it. I didn't let pride hold me back."

"No, ma'am," said Ivy June. "But Papaw taught me to want what I have, so I don't really want any new clothes. Thank you anyway."

Rosemary studied her for a few moments, and her face seemed to soften a bit. "You're welcome, Ivy June," she said finally. "And yes, John, I think I would like some of that key lime pie."

⁂

Mrs. Combs said she needed to lie down that afternoon, and Flora came over to get supper for the family.

"I *told* you not to try to put together Sunday dinner all by yourself," Flora scolded. "Why, I could have come by early and fixed that chicken. Made some biscuits."

"I'll be fine after a little nap," Catherine's mother said. "John's going to take them all to a horse farm tomorrow, and that will be my chance to rest up." Claire put her arms around her mother's neck and nestled against her, and Ivy June envied them their closeness.

"Yeah, Ivy June. You're finally going to get a chance to ride," Catherine said.

"We're going to put you on a bucking bronco!" said Peter.

Ivy June laughed. "You and Howard would get along great," she said.

March 17

I forgot it was St. Patrick's Day, but Catherine
gave me a green sweater to drape around my neck
when we went to the horse park. In the car, we were
talking about being Irish, and that's something we
have in common.

She can trace her mother's ancestors back as far
as 1710. I can't say when my relatives came to
America, but I can take you a mile up in the
hollow behind Papaw's house and show you a
little dogtrot cabin that his granddaddy built for
himself. It's half gone now, and all covered over
with weeds, but the fireplace is still there.
Mammaw said not to go in because of snakes, but I
did anyway. I stood in front of the fireplace and
thought how some of my people once stood on that
very spot. They cooked their beans and made their
corn bread and probably wondered what their
babies would do when they were grown.

If I had to give up everything I've seen and done
in Lexington so far just so I could visit the horse
park, I'd do it. There's about everything you ever
wanted to know about horses in that park—how to
care for them, what to feed them, how to groom
them, plus all about the famous horses that have
won the Kentucky Derby.

I wish I'd saved up more money for this trip,

though, because when we got to the admissions desk, I saw that I had enough to get in, but riding was extra. Mr. Combs bought the ticket for my ride. I'm eating their food, using their tickets, wearing Catherine's clothes, taking their money. . . . Seems like they're doing all the giving and me the taking. Doesn't make me feel good. Must be the way Daddy feels most of the time, taking help from Papaw.

But I did learn to ride a horse, and if Sam Feeley ever rides up to our place again with a message sent on his ham radio, I'm going to pester him for a ride!

Ivy June Mosley

CHAPTER TWENTY-TWO

March 21

Tomorrow Ivy June goes back to Thunder Creek.
A week later, Mrs. Fields will drive me to Hazard,
and somebody from Ivy June's school will meet us
there and drive me the rest of the way. Rosemary
hasn't said one more word against Ivy June and
the exchange program. I'm waiting. . . .

We've done a lot this week. We took her to Mary
Todd Lincoln's house and Old Kentucky
Chocolates. Saw the state capital and the
Lexington History Museum. There was a concert of
John Jacob Niles's songs at the university, and Ivy
June liked that a lot because she knew some of
the songs.

She liked the Kentucky Horse Park best, though. I knew she would. But she wanted to pay for her own ticket and then found she didn't have enough left for a ride—it was twenty-two dollars, I think. Dad immediately paid for her, but we knew she was embarrassed. He and Mom were talking about it, and he said he ought to have made it clear her first day here that we would pay for anything we took her to. But Mom said then the Mosleys might feel they have to pay for every place they take me when I'm in Thunder Creek, and maybe they can't afford it.

The main thing is, Ivy June finally got to ride a horse—a long ride too. We rode all around the park, and I could see how excited she was.

Mackenzie's back from Cincinnati and has been since Wednesday, but she just now called me and said we had to talk. I told her I knew what it was about. She said if I already knew, why didn't I tell her before about Andy calling me? And I said because she was my very best friend in the whole world, and I was afraid she'd be hurt if she found out.

What if it was the other way around? I asked. What if I was the one who liked Andy best, but he kept calling her? So we talked, and she said she'd already guessed that Andy was calling me before Ivy June blurted it out. What she was really upset about was that maybe I was telling Ivy June all

my secrets—about boyfriends and stuff—and I told
her that wasn't true.

I'm sorry to see Ivy June go, though. And maybe
a little scared about what it will be like living in
Thunder Creek. If there's anybody as rude to me as
Rosemary's been to her, well . . .

I wonder what she's writing in her journal about
my family. Wonder what she'll tell her mom. What
she'll tell her class. We're supposed to write down
all the ways we're different and all the ways we're
the same. I'm guessing the second list will be
longer, but who knows?

Catherine Combs

CHAPTER TWENTY-THREE

Ivy June laid out the clothes she would wear for the drive back to Thunder Creek the next morning and put the rest in her suitcase. She carefully placed the playbill from *Oklahoma!* in last. She was going to keep that forever.

She knew what was coming, because Catherine was sitting expectantly on the other bed, hands in her lap. And when the suitcase closed with a snap, Catherine said, "Okay. Now. The secret."

Ivy June, still in her pajamas, sat down across from her, pulling a corner of the spread over her legs for comfort. "All right," she said, "and no one in the whole world knows it except you, not even Shirl."

Catherine waited.

Ivy June took a deep breath. "Remember that mine accident I told about in class?"

123

Catherine nodded. "Where the men were trapped and it was all night before they were rescued?"

"Yes. Well, not everybody was alive."

Catherine's eyes grew wide.

"We just knew there was a cave-in. We didn't know if rock had fallen on anybody, whether the miners were trapped or dead. We waited and waited to hear if the rescuers had found anybody, and finally they sent up word that at least some of the men were still alive. But they wouldn't give out any names."

"That must have been awful!" said Catherine.

Ivy June nodded and steeled herself to continue: "This was last year, only a month after I'd gone to live with Mammaw and Papaw, and I was really liking it there. We all had the worry about the mine and what could happen—that's just the way we live in Thunder Creek— but this time, for me, the worry was something fierce. I prayed to God that if anybody had to die, it wouldn't be Papaw. I knew there were other men in there who were loved by their families, though, same as I loved my grandfather. So then I figured Luke Weller's daddy would be missed the least, because I knew he got ugly when he was drinking, and Luke told me he drank a lot on Saturday nights. So I prayed to God that if he had to take somebody, he'd take George Weller."

Catherine said nothing, so Ivy June barreled on.

"And then—when the missing men were found and only one was dead—Mr. Weller—I didn't know whether to thank Jesus or ask him to forgive me. And now that I've seen what a misery it's been for Luke's big family—they can hardly get by—the worry's been worse. One of Luke's sisters is on drugs and a brother's in jail. It might be that because of my selfishness, God's going to teach me a lesson, and the next person he takes will be Papaw."

"No!" Catherine said. "You can't believe God would do that, Ivy June!"

"He made it be George Weller, didn't he?"

"Luke's father could have died before you ever prayed that prayer!"

"We don't know that. Maybe it happened after I prayed," Ivy June argued, hoping all the while that Catherine was right.

"You're not that powerful, Ivy June! Just because you pray for something doesn't make it happen!"

"When Grandmommy was sick with the flu last year and I prayed for her, she got better!" Ivy June insisted. "Don't you believe in God, Cat?"

"Yes, but I don't believe he does every little thing people ask him to do. That's like . . . like magical thinking. That even though God already knew who was going to die, you could make him change his mind. And I certainly don't believe he kills people just to teach somebody a lesson!"

Ivy June didn't know whether to be relieved or skeptical. She nervously traced one finger over the weave in the bedspread. "After Papaw was rescued and Mammaw told him how much I'd cried, the next time he went in the mine he brought me out a little rock. Told me to hold it in my hand next time I worried, see how hard it was. Said to remember that he's as strong and solid as that rock."

Ivy June hunched her shoulders and was quiet for a minute. Then, "I keep praying for Papaw to live so he can retire from the mine and breathe mountain air, not coal dust. But other people have prayed for their fathers and grandfathers too, and some of those men didn't make it. Papaw's been in the mine now longer than anybody else, so chances are—"

Catherine interrupted. "Chances are he's careful and he's going to come out just fine!"

"Unless God wants to make me pay . . ."

"If God wants to make you pay, he'll let you fall off a ladder and break your neck, Ivy June, but he won't kill your grandfather!" Catherine said firmly. Then she added, "But in case you're worrying about me telling your secret, I'm not going to tell anyone else what you told me."

"Then you're a better friend than I've been to you," said Ivy June.

"Hey, we're only halfway through the exchange program," Catherine said. "You may hate me when it's over." And then she added, "Don't forget to pack your pajamas." That made them both laugh.

〰

The following day, Ivy June said goodbye to Peter and Claire and Mr. and Mrs. Combs and Catherine. Everyone hugged her, and Flora took pictures of them together on the wide front porch. Then Mrs. Fields came by in her green car, with *Buckner Academy for Girls* in silver on the driver's door, and Ivy June climbed inside.

$$\infty$$

It was Daddy who met her at the library in Hazard, not Papaw. He was parked outside the building, and walked over to get her suitcase.

"Mrs. Fields, this is my daddy," Ivy June said, having learned from Catherine that you always introduce the woman first, unless the man is somebody very old or very famous.

"How do," her father said, and shook the hand of the tall woman, who had removed her sunglasses and was smiling at him.

"We so enjoyed having your daughter with us at Buckner," Mrs. Fields said.

"I 'spect she enjoyed herself some too," Mr. Mosley answered.

"Oh, I did," said Ivy June. "And Catherine's really nice."

"You'll see her again in a week," Mrs. Fields said. "Goodbye, dear. I hope Catherine's visit with you will go as well as yours with us. It was a pleasure meeting you, Mr. Mosley."

"Same here."

Ivy June's father carried the old yellow suitcase to the

pickup truck and heaved it over the side. Ivy June climbed into the passenger seat and pulled the door closed.

Mr. Mosley started the engine.

They rode almost a block before any more words were spoken. Ivy June wanted so much to ask why Papaw hadn't come to pick her up, and cast sideways glances at her daddy to see if there was worry on his face. There didn't appear to be, however, and she knew if she asked about Papaw, it would show her disappointment that it had been Daddy waiting for her instead of him.

She also wanted to see if her daddy would start the conversation, wondering if it was always going to be she who said the first words, consciously comparing him now to Catherine's father. What would Catherine think of this quiet man who had never worn a suit in his life? Who had never praised her that she could remember, and who got so little praise himself? Who thought so little of himself, probably, for having to depend on his father to support the family.

Ivy June wondered how it could be that she and her daddy had so few things to say to each other. Was it because she was living at Papaw's now, or had it always been like this?

He did, after a while, speak first. "So . . ."

Ivy June waited, her eyes straight ahead.

They drove another few blocks. When they came to a stoplight, her father mused, with a smile, "Don't look any different."

"Didn't expect me to, did you?" she asked.

"Wasn't sure," he answered.

"Well, I saw different things . . . learned different stuff. Saw a horse farm, for one thing."

He smiled wryly this time. "Got to go all the way to Lexington to see a horse? Never saw Sam Feeley's?"

"Had to go all the way to *ride* one. Mr. Feeley never offered me a ride," Ivy June said.

"Didn't know you wanted one," her daddy said.

"Guess you never asked," she replied.

Still more silence. She was being unfair, she knew. Why should he have to guess at what she might feel or need? Did he have to do all the asking? When could his asking stop and her telling begin?

"Went to the opera house one night," she told him finally. "It's got a thousand seats, all of them red velvet. It was a musical, *Oklahoma!* You've probably heard some of the songs."

"Don't know," said her daddy.

"Never heard 'Oh, What a Beautiful Mornin''?"

"Why don't you sing it for me?"

Ivy June blinked. She could never remember a time in her life that her daddy had asked her to sing for him. She wasn't even sure that this wasn't the first time she'd ever been alone with him in a car, not even Jessie along.

"Okay," she said, and began. *"There's a bright golden haze . . ."* They had reached the state highway now, and Ivy June sang the chorus loud and clear. Sang to the trees with their feathery beginnings, the countryside, the long grass tinged blue. *"Oh, what a beautiful mornin' . . ."* She sang two verses, forgetting whether there was a third.

"That's a pretty song," her daddy said when she'd finished.

Ivy June took a chance: "I missed you. Did you miss me? Even a little?"

The pause was so long she was afraid he'd say no. But finally he said, "I wondered if you'd be all right there in Lexington with folks you don't know. But I guessed if anyone could figure out how to handle things, it was you."

Ivy June recognized this for what it was—a compliment from her daddy. It might not have been all that she wanted, but it was a start.

୧୧୨

Papaw, Ivy June discovered, had taken Howard and Ezra up near the ridge to get some pokeweed for a salad, and some sassafras bark. Ma was up at Mammaw's with Danny, helping make supper.

Daddy parked the pickup at the footbridge and carried the suitcase across and on up the hollow to Mammaw's. Tomorrow was Easter Sunday, and the Buck Run Baptist Church held a potluck dinner right after the service. Ivy June had been going to church with Mammaw and Papaw since she'd moved in with them, but her parents had stopped attending years ago, when Ma's teeth went bad. Howard went to a Sunday school in the next hollow with a friend from school. A neighbor picked up both Howard and Ezra on Sunday mornings, and Ma was glad for some peace and quiet.

Since the family wouldn't be together for Sunday dinner, Mammaw had decided to have the meal there this evening. No one called it a "welcome home" dinner, even though Ivy June suspected it was, because her family—all but Mammaw and Papaw—hadn't thought she should go away in the first place.

Mammaw's hug was warm, and the sparkle in her eyes was all Ivy June needed to know she was loved. But when Ivy June reached out for her mother, the hug Ma gave in return was a sideways sort of embrace on her way to the stove. *If you've come back with a swelled head, you can forget it,* the weak hug seemed to say.

"Jessie's got promoted to the day shift at the factory" were her mother's first words. "After three years, it's about time. Now if I can just keep her away from Harlan on Friday nights."

Jessie, Jessie, always Jessie, Ivy June thought.

"But you want her to meet somebody, don't you, Ma?" she said.

"Not anyone from the Tic Toc, I don't," Ma answered. "She don't need going to no bar."

Danny ran in just then from the back room, and Ivy June swooped him up, giving him a loud smacking kiss on the cheek.

Grandmommy, of course, was all smiles, even though she couldn't see; she kept her face turned toward the sound of Ivy June's voice.

"She's back from Lexington, Grandmommy," Mammaw told her.

The old woman groped for Ivy June's hand, and when she finally latched on, she said, "I've stayed all my life . . . right back in the mountains. I wouldn't . . . live in Lexington . . . if you give it to me and made me keep it."

"And everybody loves you being right here," Ivy June told her.

Around four, Papaw came home with the two older boys, each carrying buckets of greens and some sassafras bark. Ivy June went out on the porch to meet them, her arms open wide for Ezra. Then she hugged Papaw, squeezing him tight, and finally—his face bashful—Howard.

"What you guys been up to while I was gone?" she asked as they trooped into the house and handed their buckets to Mammaw.

"I caught a fish last week!" Ezra told her. "Howie helped me put a worm on a hook and . . ."

"And we ate it!" Danny finished for him.

"Good for you!" Ivy June said.

Howard had stories to tell of all he had done during mud vacation, and how the creek had come within six inches of the footbridge, and how Kenny Holland's go-cart had gone over the bank and gotten carried downstream.

"And Howard trapped a raccoon!" said Ezra.

"A raccoon!" Ivy June exclaimed.

"He's got the fool thing in that rusty old dog kennel back of the house," said Daddy, "feeding it scraps."

"I find out you're feeding it anything but garbage, I'll take a switch to you," Ma said to Howard. "You got one week to let that creature go!"

Howard only grinned.

At the pump by the sink, Ivy June's ma was washing the pinkish sassafras roots and scraping off shavings into a pan. Before long, the water was boiling and the sassafras gave off its root-beer fragrance. Ten minutes later, they all held cups of steaming sassafras tea sweetened with honey and let the steam warm their faces.

Jessie came up the hill about five with a shopping bag from Walmart, tired from her shopping trip, and gave Ivy June a hug.

"You buy yourself a nice shirt?" her mother asked.

In answer, Jessie held up a pair of skinny stretch pants and, ignoring her mother's exasperated look, slipped them back in the bag. "How'd it go in Lexington?" she asked Ivy June. "Where'd you go for the haircut?"

"Nowhere. Girls did it for me."

Jessie looked surprised. "They don't go to some fancy salon?"

"I don't know. But that night they were trimming hair, so I let 'em do mine."

Later, as the family gathered around the table and feasted on Mammaw's white beans and ham and Ma's corn pudding, Ivy June told them about the one-thousand-seat theater with the red velvet cushions, how she'd walked inside the Capitol, set foot in the very house

133

where Abraham Lincoln's wife was born, and gone on a forty-five-minute ride around the Kentucky Horse Park, holding the reins herself, nobody in the saddle with her.

Jessie wasn't much interested in the horse park. "What's Catherine's family like?" she asked. "They have a big house?"

Ivy June described it, not mentioning the number of bathrooms. She described each member of the Combs family, all but Rosemary, knowing that either Ma or Jessie would fasten on tight to Rosemary all the worst things they believed about city folk.

"I like Catherine's friends, too," Ivy June said. "Not all of them, but they're just like girls here. I like her two best friends a lot, Hannah and Mackenzie."

"Mackenzie!" exclaimed Jessie. "What kind of a name is that? Give a girl her mother's last name and you know for sure she's city. You'd never find a girl around here named Mackenzie."

"Well, if there weren't any differences, there wouldn't be any point in goin' up there, would there?" said Papaw, passing around the biscuits.

"We're more alike than we are different," Ivy June said earnestly, wanting her family to be kind to Catherine when she came. But inwardly, she hoped she could still say this after Catherine had been here for two weeks.

CHAPTER TWENTY-FOUR

At Buck Run Baptist, Pastor Gordon was a little late, having preached at another small church that morning, with still a third to go on his circuit. A six-foot-high wooden cross had been set up at the front of the room, held in place by a Christmas tree holder. And everyone knew that each car in the clearing out front had a Styrofoam ice chest or a plastic Playmate in its trunk, and that in those chests were casseroles and Jell-O salads and desserts, all waiting to be brought inside after the preaching.

No one dressed up much for Easter. Some of the older women, like Mammaw, came in their usual Sunday dresses, and a few of the men wore ties. There was a superstition, though, that if you didn't wear new clothes on Easter, bad luck would follow, so many of the worshippers came in at least one thing new to them, though it might have been handed down six times from one relative to the next. But mostly the forty or so members of the congregation were simply well scrubbed and brushed and combed, with every member of their household in attendance. On Easter morning there were four persons to a hymnal, not three, but so many—Ivy June among them—knew the words, they didn't even have to look at the pages.

When she and Mammaw and Papaw sang out the chorus of the final hymn,

> *Up from the grave He arose,*
> *With a mighty triumph o'er His foes. . . ."*

Ivy June let her voice soar:

> *"He arose, He arose,*
> *Hallelujah! Christ arose!"*

She wouldn't be surprised if people heard them all the way to Hazard, so enthusiastic was their singing.

At the final "Amen," while the adults greeted and hugged each other, children turned their eyes toward the back of the room, where the two church deacons were setting up a long folding table, and a woman waited with a white paper cloth to cover it.

In and out the grown-ups went, and within minutes, the table was covered with platters of fried chicken, deviled eggs, sliced ham, navy beans, scalloped potatoes, and four layer cakes, so that almost every square inch of it was occupied.

Ivy June followed Papaw in line, and when she'd filled her plate, she took it over to the row of folding chairs along one side. Back at Mammaw's house, Jessie was caring for Grandmommy, as she did every Sunday morning, so Ivy June and her grandparents could take their time.

Pastor Gordon went around the room shaking hands.

"Welcome back, Ivy June," he said. "Did you bring some new and exciting ideas with you?"

"Don't know about that, but I left a few myself," Ivy June said, and Mammaw chuckled appreciatively.

At that moment Ivy June's eye caught someone grinning at her from across the room. Jimmy Harris, a heaping plate propped on one knee, was motioning to the empty seat beside him.

Ivy June instantly felt the blood rush to her face, as it always did when the eighth grader noticed her.

What are you doing here? she mouthed in surprise.

What? he mouthed back, and pointed insistently to the empty chair.

"Someone from school," Ivy June told her grandparents, and carried her plate across the floor. "Never saw you here before," she said, sitting down by Jimmy.

"I heard they were having potluck," he said, and grinned again as he took a bite of biscuit spread with honey.

She stared at him. "I'll bet you didn't even hear the sermon, Jimmy Harris!"

He laughed then. "Did too! My aunt said she's seen you here, and asked me to come along."

"Well, hallelujah for that," Ivy June said.

"Figured this was one way to make you talk to me," he said, and his skinny knee bobbed up and down, the plate held firmly in place by one thumb.

"What do you mean, I don't talk?"

"Hello. Goodbye. That's about it," he complained.

"So what do you want me to say?"

"Heck! Didn't they teach you any manners up in Lexington?" Jimmy said. "Polite conversation?"

Ivy June gave him a broad smile. "Why, Jimmy Harris, what a pleasure seeing you here this morning. I surely hope you enjoy my grandmother's biscuits," she said sweetly.

"Now, that's better," he told her.

◎

"So what's she like?" Shirl asked on the bus Monday, when Ivy June climbed on with one of Mammaw's ham sandwiches in her lunch bag with some jelly beans that Ezra had been given at Sunday school.

"Same as us, not so different," said Ivy June.

"Fancy clothes, I'll bet. Brand-name underpants and all," Shirl prodded.

"I wouldn't know. I didn't peek. What did *you* do on vacation?"

"Went to Earl's store three nights!" Shirl said, her eyes twinkling. "You should have been there. Jimmy Harris kept looking around for you."

"He did not. He knew I was away."

"He was looking just the same."

"Looking at *you*, probably!" Ivy June teased. "Bet you wore that sweater with two baseballs in your bra."

Shirley's lips stretched into a wide smile. "Danced with Fred Mason," she said. "And we sat out behind Earl's with a Mountain Dew and I let him kiss me. A *kiss* kiss, not the skim-milk kind."

"I *said* that's what you'd be doing," Ivy June laughed as the bus stopped at Devil's Branch Road, and three kids with their collars turned up climbed aboard.

"Bet they don't do much kissing in Lexington, everything so prim and proper," said Shirl, and glanced over at Ivy June. "Catherine have a boyfriend?"

"You'd have to ask *her*," said Ivy June. "She goes to a girls' school, remember."

"Wonder who thought *that* one up! The whole point of getting out of bed in the morning is to flirt with the boys in your class," Shirl said.

∾

The teachers welcomed Ivy June back into their classes, but no one asked what she thought or felt about Lexington people or the way they lived. When Miss Dixon had first explained the program, she had told them that this discussion would come later, after Catherine had come to Thunder Creek. Instead, friends asked Ivy June about her teachers, her classes, her homework, what they were studying, and whether it was easy or hard.

"Did you take any of your drawings to show their art teacher?" Mrs. Sullivan asked.

"No, ma'am. Didn't think to do it," Ivy June replied, glad she had not.

But in music, she sang the Annie song for the class and wrote the words on the board. After rehearsing it a bit, the students divided into two groups and attempted to sing it. With hesitant male voices coming in too loud or too low, it didn't sound as good as it had in Lexington, but it was something Ivy June had brought back, as an ambassador should.

At Mammaw's later, Ivy June worked to make the house more presentable for Catherine. Papaw had put up the old army cot in the small room that served as Ivy June's bedroom, the room the girls would share. Of course Catherine would get the bed. But Ivy June began to worry how Catherine would feel about washing up at the kitchen sink in the mornings, or taking a bath in the tin washtub out on the back porch. How she might feel about tramping across wet grass mornings and evenings to use the outhouse or—worse yet—pulling the chamber pot (the slop jar, Mammaw called it) out from under the bed in the middle of the night, removing its white enameled lid, and squatting down over the pot to save a walk to the outhouse in the dark. Perhaps Ivy June should have warned her.

Strange, she thought, how you can be so used to something you just accept it. Used to washing up under your arms and around your neck while a teakettle whistled on the big iron stove to one side and the aromas of soap and oatmeal and flapjacks filled the room.

She wondered how Catherine would feel about the worn, food-stained pot holders Mammaw hung on one side of the stove. The coal-darkened fingernails of Papaw, his missing tooth, the sounds of his scrubbing or belching or sometimes cussing about something out on the back porch. In Lexington everything seemed so tidy, so formal, so clean, so perfect. . . . Then she remembered Peter's antics and Claire's curiosity and Rosemary's biting comments and knew that it wasn't—that families were imperfect in different ways.

"Missed you, granddaughter," Papaw said one evening when Ivy June was singing as she washed the stew pan. "That Lexington girl—she sing like you?"

"She sings at school. I didn't hear her much around the house," said Ivy June.

"You get a taste of life you can't forget?" her grandfather asked, giving her a sideways glance.

"You don't have to work at forgetting something if you don't want it in the first place," she answered, and that seemed to make him happy.

But there were things she did want, Ivy June discovered as she lay in bed listening to the distant sound of the creek. She sure wouldn't fight an indoor bathroom, for one. A pretty pair of shoes to wear with a dress. She'd like to have a class with as many computers as they had at Buckner, and she would love a ride to school in a car each morning instead of walking a mile or so to a bus stop, then waiting fifteen or twenty minutes for the bus to get there.

These were the small things, however. She would love a daddy like Catherine's, who asked about her day, inspected her homework. A ma who reached over to rub her back or kiss her good night, as Catherine's mom did. A family who encouraged

141

her to broaden herself and told her how well she was doing when she tried something new. Being at Catherine's house had made her even more grateful to be living with Papaw and Mammaw, but it pointed out all the more clearly just what she had been missing back at the house with Ma and Daddy. It made her feel guilty that she was special to Mammaw and Papaw, and sad for Howard and Ezra and Danny.

〰️

For the next few days, when Ivy June stopped by her ma's after school, she stayed an hour or more and made herself useful, hemming up a pair of Howard's outgrown pants for Ezra, scrubbing the worn linoleum in the kitchen, pushing Danny on the bag swing hanging from the beech tree, or—most hated job—breaking open the hardened lima bean pods that the family had picked the summer before and let dry in the sun. Even though she had put batches of them in an old pillowcase and stomped on it, many of the pods hadn't split open. Their sharp points pricked her fingers as she tried to extract the beans, but she managed to shell half a bag before it was time to go back to Mammaw's and read to Grandmommy.

On this particular day, however, Grandmommy wanted to talk, not to be read to. Not even her birthday message. She was holding one of the postcards Ivy June had sent instead.

"They nice to you, Ivy June . . . in the city?" she asked. "Or they . . . goin' s'fast . . . they ain't got time . . . to take up with you?"

"Most of the time they were nice," Ivy June told her. "Had plenty of time for me."

"I hear . . . you knock on a city folk's door . . . they don't even ask you . . . to come in," Grandmommy wheezed. "You got to . . . stand right there . . . and tell 'em what you want. And goodbye? They come to visit . . . and they take it in their minds to go . . . they jus' up and say goodbye . . . no ifs, ands, or buts. Why . . . you say goodbye to me . . . it'd be a while 'fore I let you . . . out the door. But those city folk . . . they value their time more'n . . . they value their neighbor."

Ivy June smiled. "Well, they treated me fine, Grandmommy. And I know you'll be nice to Catherine when she comes."

"She don't quarrel us out . . . I 'spect we'll git along," said Grandmommy.

※

The following afternoon, as Ivy June was dusting the windowsill above Ma's sink, lifting the accumulated bric-a-brac and wiping off the collected dirt and grime, her mother asked, "Why are you after every little speck? Don't know why you're beautifying our place. Not as though that Catherine girl was staying here."

"No, but we'll be coming by now and then," Ivy June said. "I want you all to meet her."

"Well, don't think I'll be changin' my clothes and sittin' down for a chat. There's some of us don't have maids and kitchen help, and if I got time to blow my nose, I'm doin' good," her ma said.

"I don't expect you to be anything other than you are," Ivy June told her. "I know you work hard."

"Huh!" said her ma. "Had to go all the way to Lexington to find *that* out?" She clunked a pan on the stove and dropped some hamburger meat in it.

Ivy June dusted off a little ceramic cat and set it back on the windowsill. More cheerfully, she asked, "What were you like when you were twelve, Ma?"

Ruth Mosley paused a moment, surprised at the change of subject. "Oh, like everybody else, I suppose," she said, jabbing at the meat with a fork as it began to sizzle in the pan. "We looked at movie-star magazines and thought maybe someday that would be us."

Ivy June smiled. "I sure never thought of *me* as a movie star," she said, half hoping her mother would disagree, but she didn't.

"Well," her mother continued, "most of us didn't have the sense we were born with. Figured things like that just happened. No thought at all of how to make it real."

"Yeah, who would?"

"Then Russell, he comes along—I was fifteen, he was going on twenty. He's a shy sort, see, and once I could tell he was sweet on me . . . why, what girl wouldn't go for a young man already out in the world? By then, I suppose I figured that me being a movie star wasn't about to happen, but we could still be in love like in the movies. And at fifteen, I figured that was as good as it was going to get."

Ivy June remained silent, knowing her Mother would say more.

"Day I reached sixteen, Russell and me just off and got ourselves married. Jessie come along about a year later, and that's the story of my life." She picked up the shaker and generously salted the hamburger.

"I don't know about *that*," Ivy June said. "There's a few more kids to account for." She pulled out a chair then and sat down, waiting for the rest of the story.

Her mother sighed. "And one I lost between you and Jessie. Never knew that, did you? Miscarriage. But once your children come along, you can kiss your other plans goodbye." She stopped suddenly when she noticed Ivy June's startled face. "You know," she said, "those are the same exact words my ma said to me after my three sisters were born."

Ivy June felt moisture in her eyes. "And how do you suppose it makes *me* feel?" she said, her voice trembling.

Mrs. Mosley put down the fork and sat across from Ivy June. This time her voice as well as her face had softened. "Same way I felt when I heard it from my ma, I suppose. I'm sorry. My movie-star dreams, that's all I meant. Sometimes life just pushes out words better kept inside."

Ivy June blinked back tears. "You could have done something else, though. Why *didn't* you finish high school?" She glanced shyly at her mother, then down at her hands. "There's ways to get your diploma, even after you're married."

"I did go back for a semester. But then I got pregnant, Russ took sick—his lungs, you know—and he only worked off and on at the lumberyard. I had to get me a job as cashier at the Stop-and-Go, and that was the end of my schooling. Papaw built us this house here in the hollow. I suppose we never would have made it without him."

Ivy June didn't answer. It was hard in the mountains, but some people made it. Miss Dixon had made it. The preacher had made it. The manager of the Walmart down in Harlan, the librarian up at Hazard. But of course, not everyone married into sickness. Not everyone had babies right away.

Her mother must have sensed what she was feeling, because she suddenly reached across the table for Ivy June's hand and gave it an affectionate little shake. "It don't have to happen to you, Ivy June," she said. "You take care and see that it don't. And don't go tellin' your brothers any of this. Shirl, neither."

"Jessie knows, doesn't she?"

"About the miscarriage, not my dreams. Jessie never seems to stand up for herself. Didn't ever ask for the day shift till they up and gave it to her. Compares herself to everyone else and always comes up short. I get tired, sometimes, keepin' others down just so Jessie'll seem taller herself."

Ivy June sat wordless, astonished. Did Ma even realize what she'd said? Despite her attention to Jessie, maybe it wasn't the older daughter Ma thought of as an example for the boys. Could Ma possibly be jealous of *her*?

If only Ma knew how shaky Ivy June felt some of the time. If only she knew how Ivy June had compared herself to Catherine, her family to Catherine's, and how nervous she was about Catherine's coming here.

CHAPTER TWENTY-FIVE

The Saturday Catherine was to arrive, Grandmommy was upset. Ivy June had hidden the worn slippers with the hole in the toe and the soles coming apart. She had taken the new slippers Jessie had given Grandmommy last Christmas and tried to put them on the old woman's feet.

Grandmommy couldn't see what was happening, but she obviously felt something different.

"Them ain't the ones!" she cried, kicking at the hands that were trying to guide them on.

"They're prettier on your feet, Grandmommy!" Ivy June insisted. "They make you look like a princess with those little bows on their tops."

"Take 'em off!" Grandmommy wailed. "Take 'em off!"

Mammaw came to the door of the room, where

Grandmommy sat on the side of the daybed, thin legs dangling.

"Ivy June, will you stop aggravatin' that woman!" she scolded. "She starts out like this in the morning, she'll be all nerves by afternoon. And her with a sore toe."

Ivy June reluctantly put the new slippers back in the box. "Just wanted her to look nice," she said.

"What you've been tryin' to do this past week is make us change our ways, and I guess we got Lexington to thank for that. 'Put on a different apron, Mammaw!' 'Let me give you a manicure, Papaw!' 'Can't we toss out that old frayed rug?' All we've been hearin' from you is making things different. They was good enough for us a month ago and way many years before that, so they're good enough for us now."

Ivy June listened, her face warm with embarrassment. Mammaw's words felt like sandpaper against her ears. Was that the way it was in the mountains? If it was good enough once, it was good enough always? Never a need for change?

"I thought you *wanted* me in that exchange program" was all she managed to say.

Mammaw was still angry as she retrieved Grandmommy's old slippers and slid them on the elderly woman's feet. "Wanting you to see how other people live their lives isn't the same as wanting you to turn us inside out. Maybe you ought to go up into the mountains awhile and get your head on straight. Give us some peace."

Stung, Ivy June turned away and went to the kitchen, thinking there would at least be a few kind words from Papaw. But he silently ate his oatmeal, eyes on the bowl, and she fled out the door, letting the screen bang behind her.

What had she been thinking, letting a Lexington girl come here? It would have been better if Catherine had come to Thunder Creek first, before Ivy June had seen the Combses' house with the polished floors and the linen tablecloths, before she'd shared Catherine's room with the white shutters, the matching curtains and spread, and a computer in the corner. Better for Ivy June to be humiliated later in Lexington in front of people she didn't know than to be embarrassed in front of family.

She started up the path in such turmoil that the wind didn't bother her; it helped her cool down. But as the path grew steeper and she slowed, the wind tossed her hair and she wished she'd worn a jacket. She couldn't go back now. And when she got to the Whistling Place, she sat beneath the three saplings, which were still leafless, and hugged herself, hands gripping her upper arms.

Down below, through the bare branches, she could see at least halfway up the hollow—the long stretch of field between Papaw's and the few houses up near Vulture's Pass, land used for farming in summer. And then, in the opposite direction, her family's little tin-roofed house, close to the swinging bridge.

Across Thunder Creek, where a road came winding

through, the hills seemed to go on forever, layer after layer, with mist rising among them. Their cover of leafless trees appeared ghostly gray, but the tips of the branches had turned a faint lavender-pink, the first whisper of spring.

Wheeeeooooo, the wind whistled in Ivy June's ears. A crow glided by over the hollow, its wings barely moving. From somewhere behind her, farther up, a blue jay gave a territorial warning, and sparrows gossiped from a bush nearby.

Ivy June sat still as a rock, watching the valley below come to life on a Saturday morning: a car moving slowly on the road beyond the creek; a man in a field, attacking weeds with a hoe; shadows of clouds sweeping across the valley floor.

Cautiously, taking its time, the sun edged out from behind a cloud, and the landscape grew lighter, then brighter still, until suddenly the sun was out full, warming Ivy June's face and arms, and the dew on the grass around her shimmered like beads of glass.

Was the opera house any grander than this? Ivy June asked herself. Could one thousand red-cushioned seats upstage the Whistling Place in early spring, with the countryside coming to life around her as far as the eye could see? Was even the front-row balcony as grand as this, the very edge of the ridge, where you could look down like God himself, almost, seeing everything?

A half hour later, her heart quiet, her face calm, Ivy

June got up, brushed the dry leaves from her jeans, and started back down to Mammaw's.

After making Papaw's favorite grilled cheese sandwich for him at noon and cleaning up the kitchen, Ivy June went down to Ma's. Daddy was on a ladder, nailing up a sheet of tin that had come loose from the roof during the heavy rains a few weeks back. Howard was holding the ladder steady.

"What time's she comin', Ivy June?" Howard called when he saw her.

"Sometime around three. That's all they told me," she replied. "We'll know when we see her." Ivy June went on inside and Ezra immediately cried, "Is she here?"

"Not yet," said Ivy June.

"You'd think this was a circus coming, all the excitement," said Ma.

"It'll be a circus, all right," said Jessie, who was sitting on the old swaybacked couch polishing her nails. "Whole project's a circus, you ask me."

Ivy June was determined to ignore her. If she could deal with Rosemary, then Catherine could deal with Jessie. Sure would be interesting to get those two women together. Send them off on a trip or something. Alaska, maybe.

Ma seemed determined to ignore Jessie's remark too. Despite her previous complaining, she had put on a clean shirt today, and had changed from those baggy-kneed sweatpants into a more presentable pair.

"The boys are begging to carry her suitcase up to Mammaw's," she said.

"Fine with me, long as they don't go looking inside," Ivy June said. She sat down at the end of the couch, careful not to bounce and disturb the nail polishing. "How do you like working the day shift now?" she asked her sister.

"Sure took 'em long enough to let me have it," Jessie said. "But it's nice to have my evenings free. Not that there's anything much to do with them, except drive on down to the Tic Toc."

"Shirl and Fred Mason were dancing out in the parking lot at Earl's store over vacation," Ivy June hinted, "and she said *lots* of folks came by."

"Yeah, well, Shirl's going on thirteen and I'm going on twenty, so it's a whole lot of difference there," said Jessie, blowing on one hand, then giving her attention to the other.

"I keep tellin' her about this supper club I hear they got up at Hazard. Barbecue place with live country music on weekends," said Ma. "All for the price of supper. And a nice kind of people who come."

"Yeah, I'll feel real fine sitting there all by myself like I've never been asked out in my whole life," said Jessie.

"You get up some girlfriends and go, Jessie Mosley!" Ma said impatiently. "You don't sit around here waitin' for some Prince Charming to ride up and carry you off. You wait for that, and next thing you know, you'll run off with the first man smiles your way at the Tic Toc. Get up a crowd of girlfriends and go have yourselves a good time. Meet different people. The Deep Well Harley Boys, that's the name of the band going to play on weekends."

Jessie grunted. "Next you'll be wanting me to go to Lexington."

"Don't put words in my mouth," Ma snapped. Then, more earnestly, "There's more to you than you realize, Jessie Anne. You meet some nice people, see what they've done with their lives, give you some ideas."

"Yeah, I move out of here with my paycheck, *then* what'll you do?" Jessie asked.

"Then we'll cope," Ma said determinedly. "We'll *cope,* Jessie. But I want you to have a chance. And maybe we oughtn't be so hard on people who are tryin' to broaden themselves."

"Well . . . maybe," Jessie said.

ᘒ

"She's here!"

The screen squeaked when Howard stuck his head inside, then banged as he raced off down to the footbridge.

Ezra and Danny came running from the kitchen, where they'd been eating crackers spread with peanut butter, and the screen door slammed again as they ran after their older brother.

And then it was Ivy June who was hurrying outside

153

and down the path to the creek, where Catherine and Miss Dixon were getting out of the car on the other side.

Catherine was looking all around her—up at the mountains, down at the creek, and then at the welcoming committee swarming toward her. Miss Dixon waved at Ivy June, then pulled Catherine's bag from the trunk, while Catherine reached for the two smaller bags in the backseat. It was obvious she had brought more clothes with her than Ivy June owned in her whole closet.

"Hi, Ivy June!" Catherine called.

"You've got yourself your own personal porters," Ivy June called back, smiling. "They want to carry your bags on up to Mammaw's."

"I'll carry the big one till we cross the creek," Miss Dixon told Howard as three pairs of hands reached for it. "How you guys doing? Everything all set for your visitor?"

"We're ready and waiting," Ivy June said, giving Catherine a hug. "Catherine, the tallest here is Howard, then Ezra, and this little fellow is Danny. Miss Dixon already knows them."

Howard gave a shy smile, a lock of brown hair hanging down over his eyes; Ezra, the round one, grinned broadly, arms dangling at his sides; while Danny beamed up at Catherine, his chubby cheeks dimpled, eyes squinting in the sun.

"Hello, hello, hello," Catherine said. "I'll get your names straight after a bit."

Howard took the two smaller bags Catherine was carrying and swaggered as he crossed the swinging bridge to show he didn't even have to hold on. Catherine followed hesitantly as the bridge swayed and jiggled with each step. Gripping the cable that served as a handrail, she managed to get across and said, laughing, "Guess I'll get used to that, too, after a bit!"

On the other side, Ezra and Danny each grabbed for one of Howard's bags, and Howard politely took the large suitcase from the teacher.

"Well, is there anything else I can do to help you get settled?" Miss Dixon asked the girls.

"I don't think so, ma'am," Ivy June said. "The boys'll walk her bags on up the hill, but we're going to stop at Ma's house first."

"Okay, then," said her teacher. "I'll see you at school on Monday. We're really looking forward to having you with us, Catherine."

"I'm excited too!" said Catherine. "Thanks a lot for the ride."

As Miss Dixon's car went back up the winding road on the other side of the creek, Catherine said, "Wow! This is pretty country. Would you believe I've never been south of Lexington? Not really."

"Then I hope you like mountains, because that's about all we've got," said Ivy June, her brothers hanging close to listen in.

"And snakes!" said Howard mischievously, holding

the large suitcase in front of him with both hands, so that it banged against his shins.

"And bears!" said Ezra, puffing his way up the bank. "I seen a black bear once!"

"Me too!" piped up Danny.

"Well, I'll be careful of snakes and bears, then," said Catherine, and grinned at Ivy June.

Russell Mosley came around the house, hammer in hand, and stopped when he saw Catherine. "Reckon this is the new girl," he said, and gave his shy smile. "Stayin' two weeks, huh? Place should pretty up some while you're here."

"Catherine, this is my dad," said Ivy June.

"I think it's pretty already," Catherine told him. "I saw some of those big yellow flowers that grow in ditches . . . what are they called?"

"There's a name for 'em, but I just call 'em swamp flowers. Saw some myself yestiddy when I was down that-away." He nodded toward the porch. "Your ma and Jessie is waiting to meet her too," he said to Ivy June.

The boys set the bags and the suitcase on the porch and followed the girls inside.

Ma came in from the kitchen and smiled at Catherine.

"You just come on in," she said. "You thirsty, Catherine? Want some apple juice?"

"This is my mom," said Ivy June.

"Thank you, but Miss Dixon gave me some Sprite in

156

the car. I'm fine, really," Catherine said, and shook Ma's hand.

"Well, this here is Jessie," said Ma, stepping aside so that Catherine could get a look at the young woman on the couch. Jessie, a magazine on her lap, was still blowing on one set of nails.

"Hello," said Catherine.

"This is my sister," said Ivy June.

"Nice to meet you," said Jessie. "Long drive down?"

"Not so long. Once we got to Hazard, it was only an hour more," Catherine answered.

"Well, it doesn't seem fair that Ivy June got one week of school up in Lexington and one week of vacation, but you've got to do two weeks of school," Jessie said.

"I know," Catherine said, laughing. "Something to do with when the schools take spring break, I guess."

"Makes it seem like one week of school in Lexington is all Thunder Creek kids can take," Jessie added, and Ivy June's face flushed with embarrassment.

But Catherine said, "No, it depends where Easter falls, for one thing, and when testing begins."

Fortunately, Ruth Mosley interrupted. "Our Jessie works at the sweatshirt factory down near Harlan. Does the trim. Just got promoted to day shift."

"Congratulations!" said Catherine.

"Well, Mammaw and Papaw are waiting for us, so I guess we'd better get on up the hill," Ivy June said quickly.

"We'll see you around, then," said Jessie, and the girls

went back out, the boys skittering on ahead of them, grabbing at the suitcase and the bags they would each carry.

※

Ivy June's grandparents were both sitting on the porch when Howard and Ezra, perspiring now, hoisted their bags up onto the steps. Danny came trailing behind with the smallest bag.

"You made it!" Catherine said, smiling at him. "You are really strong, you know it?"

It took Danny two tries to get the bag up onto the step, and then he sat down and grinned.

Papaw stood up and shook Catherine's hand, enveloping it in his two large palms, which covered her hand completely.

"Welcome," he said. "Ivy June's hardly stopped talkin' 'bout you since she was up your way."

"And this is Mammaw," said Ivy June as Mammaw leaned her thin body forward and clasped Catherine's other hand. She was all smiles.

"I got lemonade and shortbread cookies, you want a snack before dinner," she offered.

"*I* want some!" said Ezra.

"Me too!" chimed in Danny.

"Well now, you all just come in here and let's see what I can find," Mammaw said, easing herself up out of the rocker. "Only two apiece, boys, 'cause I baked these special for Catherine."

The three boys eagerly pulled chairs up to the table, and Ivy June let Catherine have the fourth chair. Howard, surprisingly, got up then and let Ivy June sit down, and she smiled at this sudden gallantry in front of Catherine.

"Heeeelllllllp!" came a shaky voice from the other room. "H-help!"

Catherine started and looked around anxiously.

"It's only Grandmommy, feeling left out," Ivy June explained, getting up and heading toward the room that was now her great-grandmother's. "I'll wheel her in."

"She's a hundred years old!" said Danny soberly, nodding for emphasis, and held up all the fingers on both hands, studying them thoughtfully.

"It's ten times your fingers, Danny," Howard told him, laughing.

"Amazing!" said Catherine, and smiled as the wheelchair was pushed into the room. "I've never met anyone who was a hundred years old."

And Grandmommy, looking about for the source of the new voice, responded, "I never did neither, and . . . I can't . . . even see myself."

CHAPTER TWENTY-SIX

March 30

  I'm here at Thunder Creek and we just got back from church. Jessie came up and watched Grandmommy while the four of us rode to the Buck Run Baptist Church in Grandfather Mosley's old car. People here sure do like to sing. Makes our congregation in Lexington seem pitiful. But here they slide their voices from one note to the next—almost make a ritual of it. That will take some getting used to.

  On the drive to Thunder Creek yesterday, it was like we were going into another land almost. Seen from a distance, the mountains are knobby at the top, not pointed or rolling. If you look low out of the car window when you're actually in them, you'd think a storm was coming up, it's so dark. And then you realize it's mountainside you're looking at, and you have to raise your eyes to see the sky.

When we drive around Lexington, we see signs reading FINE ARABIAN HORSES or WILLOW BROOK FARMS. Down here the signs read BLACK DIAMOND COAL and FIREWOOD—CHEAP, and SOUP BEANS AND CORN BREAD. I'm surprised how many of the small houses have a creek between them and the road, with some kind of footbridge to cross over. Here at Thunder Creek, it's a narrow swinging bridge that jiggles and sways with each step.

Ivy June and I were too tired last night to write in our journals, so we're doing it now while Grandma Mosley fries the chicken. Ivy June says they always have fried chicken for Sunday dinner. They eat their big meal when they get home from church, just like we do at home.

There was a little welcoming committee there at the bridge when Miss Dixon drove up: Ivy June and her three brothers. The boys carried my bags all the way up the hill to where Ivy June's living with her grandparents, a quarter mile, maybe.

It's surprising how comfortable Ivy June and her family are, living with less. Her grandparents, anyway. I've lived primitively at summer camp, but

I don't know how well I'll do sharing this small house with four people. I'm glad I'm not staying down at the other house with all those brothers.

I like Ivy June even though she did cause a quarrel between Mackenzie and me. I like her grandparents, too, and even the great-grandmother's a hoot. Full of stories about growing up here in the mountains. Said she didn't have any toys as a child except for a couple of corncob dolls. Told me that she and her sisters swung from one hill to another on grapevines, and made dresses for themselves out of leaves. She even asked if my parents were divorced. Said she heard everybody in the city got divorced at one time or another. When I told her my parents were still together, she said, "That's good, then. Hiram and me, we never even studied about a divorce."

Ivy June's letting me sleep in her bed while she takes the cot. Right now she's sitting on the floor, using the cot for a desk while she writes in her journal. Her brothers hung around at dinnertime, and Mammaw—as Ivy June calls her grandmother—told them they could stay. Actually, what she said was, "Well, boys, find you some chairs and I'll put on more plates." They started dragging in every chair they could find, and a step stool, too. And she told Howard to "run down and tell your ma you're eating up here."

That's another thing—no phone. Deep in the

hollows, whenever the people in one house want to talk to the other, somebody has to be the messenger. They pray before meals like we do. The grandfather, Papaw, folds his hands in front of him and bows his head. He prayed for the Lord to bless me, their guest, and I think that's about the most welcome I ever felt anywhere.

Ivy June adores him, I can tell. He doesn't say a lot, but when he does, it's worth listening to. He's sort of a philosopher. Sees things from a different perspective.

I wish I had grandparents I loved that much. Instead, I'm stuck with Rosemary and Gramps. It's not a kind thing to say, I know, but we're supposed to express our honest thoughts in our journals, and I can't be more honest than that.

Catherine Combs

CHAPTER TWENTY-SEVEN

March 30

I'd sure like to know what Catherine's writing
about me. About here. About us. Now that she's
seen how we live, though, I don't feel as worried
as I did before.

She didn't bat an eye when I showed her the
outhouse, back in the trees. Was surprised we have
toilet seats over the holes, and that they're clean, too.
What she did blink her eyes at was the chamber
pot—the slop jar under my bed—like all of us have.

"What's that for?" she asked, lifting the lid and
looking inside. When I told her it was to use as a
toilet in the middle of the night, she looked
shocked. "I couldn't!" she said.

"Yes, you could, if you had to go bad enough," I told her. "Just put the lid on again after, and we'll empty it in the morning." Then we laughed. If I know Catherine, though, she'll hold it in till morning.

I can tell she "dressed down" to come here. Brought her oldest jeans. Left her North Face jacket at home. No shoes with the fancy heel. No panty hose. She probably doesn't want anyone at school thinking she's trying to show us up. But . . . so what? I dressed up to go to Lexington, didn't I? We both want to fit in.

I think she got along okay with Ma, but I was embarrassed to death when Ma told about Jessie getting the day shift, like she'd just been made manager at Walmart or something.

Mammaw and Papaw like Catherine, I can tell. She brought them a photography book. <u>Kentucky</u>, it says on the cover, and it's mostly photographs to show just how many different things make up our state—mountains and horse farms and rivers and parks.

"Why, look at this!" Mammaw says, pointing to Cumberland Falls. And I know I'm going to have to describe every one of those pictures to Grandmommy by and by.

Anyway, I'm breathing easier because Catherine's been nice. If she's still mad at me about that boyfriend, she doesn't show it. I notice she brought her cell phone, though. She probably didn't believe me when I told her we're in a no-service area. No "boyfriend calls" up here in the hollow.

Ivy June Mosley

CHAPTER TWENTY-EIGHT

An hour after Sunday dinner, as Ivy June and Catherine were washing the frying pan and stacking the chipped white plates on the oilcloth-covered shelves in the kitchen, they heard Mammaw call to Papaw to come look at Grandmommy's toe.

"Don't you tetch it!" Grandmommy cried. "Don't you go tetchin' that toe!"

Papaw put down the almanac he was reading and walked from the parlor into what used to be the dining room, where the one-hundred-year-old woman sat on the daybed, one foot propped up on a stool.

"Mama, your foot's swelled up again," the girls heard him tell her. "You know what Dr. Grace said about tellin' her 'fore those red streaks start travelin' up your leg."

"Jus' bring me some salt water . . . and soak it,"
Grandmommy pleaded.

The girls could hear Ivy June's grandparents talking in
low voices. "Last time Mama got to hurtin', she said she
was sufferin' so bad she'd have to get better before she
could die!" Papaw said. "I'm going for Dr. Grace."

He came striding through the kitchen and reached
for his old hat with the stained sweatband, then took
his key off the hook, went out, and started down the
hill.

"The doctor comes all the way out here?" Catherine
whispered.

"Has to. Grandmommy broke her hip once and it
never healed right. We can't get her into the car," Ivy
June explained.

"How far away is the doctor?" asked Catherine.

"About thirty miles, if she's in. If she's out making
rounds, he'll just have to find someone who's seen where
she's headed and try to catch up with her."

"But what if it was an emergency?" Catherine exclaimed.

Ivy June had no answer for that. "We do the best we
can. It's just the way we live."

Mammaw came out to the kitchen and filled a pan
with water from the teakettle, then poured a little salt in
it and stirred. "I surely did not need this trouble today,"
she murmured. "Got me a headache the size of my fist,
and I've been wanting to get to the garden and see if that
asparagus came up again this year."

"Is there anything we can do to help?" Catherine asked.

"You might check and see if her socks are dry. I washed 'em out last night and hung 'em on the porch. Ivy June, that foot look swollen yestiddy when you was tryin' to put those slippers on her feet?"

"No, ma'am. Not a lot, anyway. Not that you could notice."

"Well, it's pink as watermelon now, and there's a sore between her toes. I'll put on some of my tallow salve when we've finished the soaking and see if that'll hold her till Dr. Grace gets here."

The girls went out onto the porch and took down the white stockings flapping in the breeze.

"What's tallow salve?" asked Catherine.

"You don't want to know," said Ivy June.

"Of course I do!"

"You'd have to get all the ingredients from Mammaw, but I know it has beef fat, turpentine, camphor, and whiskey in it," Ivy June said.

"Yum!" said Catherine.

Ivy June poked her. "You don't *drink* it!" she said, and the girls laughed.

〰

It was an hour and a half later when Papaw came back with Dr. Grace. She had driven her own car as far as the footbridge, then followed him up the long hill with her worn black bag in hand. Catherine seemed astonished that the doctor was much older than Papaw. Definitely in her eighties. She stopped a few times on her way up the hill to catch her breath, then plodded on, her legs taking long strides.

"Hello there, Emma," she said to Mammaw as she came in the door. She placed her bag on the table and took off her coat. "Nice warm wind we got out there today. Crocuses are up down next to the clinic."

"That's good to hear, Dr. Grace," Mammaw said. "This here is Catherine Combs from up in Lexington. She's on the exchange program."

"Hello, Catherine," the doctor said. "And how you doing, Ivy June?"

"Doing okay," said Ivy June.

The doctor was a small woman, even thinner than Mammaw. She got right down to business, and her gnarled fingers worked efficiently at the clasp on her bag.

"Can I give you a cup of sassafras tea?" asked Mammaw.

"Wait till I see the patient," the doctor said, rolling up her sleeves and walking over to the pump at the sink. She worked the handle up and down a few times. "Find me some of that lye soap, would you?" she asked, and Mammaw slid the soap dish toward her and produced a clean towel from the cupboard.

"It's that toe again," Mammaw told her. "I got it salved up some."

"Best you let me look at it plain next time," Dr. Grace

said. "You want to go ahead and rinse it off for me, and I'll come see what's what."

Papaw put one hand on Ivy June's shoulder, the other on Catherine's, and guided them toward the front door. Behind them they could hear Dr. Grace's voice as she entered Grandmommy's room: "How you doing, Iree? It's Dr. Grace, here to look at that foot of yours."

"Don't tetch it!" Grandmommy began.

Out on the porch, Papaw sat down on the swing. "Good idea for us to just sit this one out," he said. Ivy June sat down beside him, and Catherine took the rocker.

When Grandmommy hollered—and she always hollered a lot when Dr. Grace came by—Ivy June could only imagine what was happening to her. Catherine looked alarmed.

"Not nearly as bad as it sounds," Papaw said. "Older she gets, the younger she sounds. Figure one of these days she'll have the cry of a newborn baby. It's strange, you know, to feel like a daddy to your very own mama."

"I could never be a doctor," said Catherine. "I would hate being responsible for anybody's life. I'd worry about making some huge mistake."

"They do, sometimes. No matter what kind of work you do, you make mistakes," Papaw said, pushing gently against the floorboards with his feet.

"Do you ever make mistakes in the mine?" Ivy June asked, not sure if she wanted the answer.

Papaw nodded, arms folded loosely across his chest. "Sometimes. So far I've been lucky. Either the mistakes aren't big enough to cause trouble, or somebody discovers 'em before it's too late."

"Would you want your grandsons to work in the mine?" Catherine asked him.

"That's up to them," said Papaw. "I'd have no say in it."

"Miss Dixon says we should figure out what we like to do most and what we do best, and then find a way to make a living of it," said Ivy June.

"Well, that's easy to say, girl, but it's not always possible to do. When I was eighteen and saw my four older brothers scatter to the winds—my pa was doing poorly, and there was still a brother younger than me—I went to work in the mine to help out. I didn't much like it, but the pay was good. Year or two went by, and I figured this was where I was goin' to be, 'cause I didn't see a future for myself anywhere else."

"What part didn't you like?" Catherine asked, and Ivy June knew it would probably all be recorded later in her journal.

Papaw smiled wryly. "All of it. Didn't like the way it did my back, didn't like the dark and the damp, didn't like comin' home all covered in coal soot. But the money helped out at home, and by then I had me a wife and a couple sons. I made up my mind that I would be the hardest-workin' man on a job he didn't like that the coal company had ever seen."

Ivy June listened in silence and sadness at the thought of her grandfather's going to work every day at a job he didn't like. She tried to understand the mind of the strong, quiet man, whose skin was a map of small wrinkles around his deep blue eyes. But she also knew there was a certain pride in being a miner, and it wasn't every man who had the courage and the muscle and the guts to go deep inside a hole every day, not knowing for sure whether he would walk out on his own two feet or be carried out.

"And that's where I get my satisfaction," Papaw continued. "Every day that the bell clangs and my shift is over, I tell myself I did the best work of any man in the hole. And I remind myself of it every morning. It's easy to do a good job on work you love. Hard as paddlin' upstream to do work you don't like and do it well. But I do it."

Ivy June nestled against him, her head on his shoulder. "I'll be glad when July comes and you never have to go down in the mine again. What will you tell yourself *then* when you get up in the mornings?"

Papaw grinned down at her. "I'll tell myself that now I get to do just what I want, and I can do it every which way, won't matter."

The squeaky sound of the pump handle came again from the kitchen, and a minute later Dr. Grace appeared in the doorway.

"Well, Spencer, I had to lance that foot again, but I think we've stopped the infection," she said. "She's back there giving Emma the what-for 'cause you sent for me."

Papaw smiled a little and stood up, and the girls

173

followed him inside. Mammaw came out of the next room, wiping her hands on her apron.

Dr. Grace took a large bottle out of her medicine case and counted out fourteen pills. "I want Iree to take two of these a day for a week," she said. "One in the morning and one at night."

"What about a cup of tea now, Dr. Grace?" Mammaw said.

"I appreciate it, Emma, but I've got to see Mr. Gibbons this afternoon. I pray his leg doesn't have to come off, 'cause I can't do it, and the hospital's full up."

"You'll put this visit on our bill?" Papaw asked.

"Of course. You make sure she takes those pills, Emma. It's trouble, I know. If the pill's too big, cut it in half, but make sure she swallows both halves. Don't let her fool you. If I know Iree, she's got a dozen tricks up her sleeve, and if she lives to be a hundred and one, she'll have a dozen more."

The next morning did not start out particularly well. Mammaw rapped on Ivy June's door at six o'clock, and the first thing Catherine asked was where she could wash her hair.

Ivy June climbed off the cot and turned around. "We don't have a shower," she reminded Catherine.

"I know, but I could wash it in a sink," Catherine said. And when Ivy June explained that both the pump on the back porch and the one in the kitchen produced ice-cold water, and that Mammaw used the kitchen sink in getting breakfast, Catherine asked, "But what do *you* do?"

"I do mine on the weekend when I take a bath," Ivy June said. "Mammaw heats water for me in the kettle and we add that to the water in the tub."

Catherine's face wrinkled in disgust. "But mine's all oily, and my scalp itches!" she said, running her hands through her hair. "I have to wash it every day."

"If you want, you could stand in the washtub out on the porch and I'll tip the teakettle over you, but I don't think we can do that and still make the bus," Ivy June said.

So Catherine just brushed her hair instead. After a bowl of Mammaw's oatmeal with honey and raisins, the girls put on their jackets and backpacks and set off down the hill for the bus stop.

Shirl was already on the bus when Ivy June and Catherine got on. She had saved a space in the back beside some rowdy boys so that the two girls could sit with her, but Ivy June took one look at the boys and nudged Catherine into a two-person seat by the window. In the back, Shirl gave an exasperated frown, and Ivy June turned to go talk with her.

"Y'all sit down back there," the driver barked, looking at her in his rearview mirror, his arms working to maneuver around a hairpin curve.

"We'll sit together at lunch," Ivy June called, and fell onto the seat beside Catherine as the bus lurched.

175

Catherine had her face against the glass, trying to see just how high up the mountain went.

Forty minutes later, when they got off at school, Shirl and some of the other girls gathered around Ivy June and Catherine with polite but wary smiles and greetings. Ivy June introduced them.

"This is Angela; this is Mary Beth; and this is Shirl, the one and only," she said.

"Oh, the *infamous* Shirl!" Catherine grinned.

"She been telling my life story?" Shirl asked.

"Oh, Shirl, what's to tell?" said Mary Beth.

And Angela teased, "Eat, kiss, sleep. Eat, kiss, sleep." The girls hooted, and as the bell sounded, Ivy June said, "Whoever gets to lunch first, save seats. Okay?"

♒

Miss Dixon was the most welcoming of all the teachers, Ivy June felt. One or two of the others, perhaps, might have thought that Catherine was judging them, comparing them to the private-school teachers in Lexington. But as Catherine had once said of her own family, she was nothing if not polite. And that, in the end, seemed to win the teachers over.

"This is Catherine Combs, visiting us from Buckner Academy for two weeks," Ivy June announced in each class.

"I imagine you find our school pretty different?" the substitute teacher in history asked that morning.

"No, ma'am," Catherine replied. "I'll have to study just as hard."

At lunchtime, Shirl and Angela and Mary Beth had saved a table, and Catherine looked around. "Aren't we supposed to pick up trays?"

"Don't even think it," Ivy June told her. "Mammaw would have seven fits if you ever told her you wanted school food from the cafeteria."

Catherine looked longingly at the large slices of pizza some of the other girls were eating. But she changed her mind when Ivy June opened the paper bag Mammaw had filled that morning, and produced two thick sandwiches of homemade bread filled with slices of roast chicken; little slices of dried apple sprinkled with cinnamon; and two carefully wrapped slices of chocolate cake.

"Oh, man!" she said. "I'll be so spoiled when I get back to Buckner, it'll never be the same."

"Have you always gone to private schools?" Mary Beth asked.

"I guess so. I don't remember much about kindergarten, but I've been at Buckner since first grade. It's where my mom went to school."

"Bet it's different staying at Ivy June's grandparents' place," said Shirl. "You and her squished in that one tiny room."

"Not *that* different," said Catherine. "I have to share a bathroom with my sister."

Some of the girls stopped chewing.

"A bathroom just for you and your sister?" one of them asked.

"How many bathrooms in your whole house?" asked Shirl.

Catherine appeared to be counting, and her cheeks had turned a faint pink. "Four, I guess," she said. "I mean, counting the toilet in the basement."

"Wow!" said Angela.

"So how do you like the bathroom at Ivy June's?" Shirl teased.

"Oh, I'm used to outdoor toilets," said Catherine. "I go to camp every summer."

"Yeah? Wait'll it gets warmer and the snakes come out," said Mary Beth.

"A skunk got in ours once and we couldn't use it for a week," said another girl.

"Wait'll she sees a bear some night between her and the outhouse," said Angela.

"You can't say you're used to outdoor toilets until you've lived with one through a winter," said Shirl. "Until you have to put on your coat and your boots to get through two feet of snow, and the temperature's down around zero."

"So I'll use the pot!" Catherine retorted, and the other girls laughed. But Ivy June knew how Catherine felt just then. All she had to do was remember how she herself had felt, sitting in Jennifer Paine's family room while Jennifer played the piano.

∞

CHAPTER TWENTY-NINE

March 31

I guess I'm finding it harder than I thought to
live like the Mosleys. This is the second day I've
gone without washing my hair, and already I can't
stand it.

It's hard to tell about school so far. I think Ivy
June's friends are waiting to see me fall on my
face. But I made them laugh at lunchtime, and
after that they warmed up a little.

As for the teachers, some are better than others.
The classes don't seem to have the discussions we
have at Buckner. It's pretty much teachers doing
the talking and students doing the homework. But
here they know their part of the country better than

we know Lexington. They can tell you the name of every river or school or church or valley—the owner of every house within miles of their own. Ask them when the river flooded or where was the last big fire, and they'll tell you. I don't even know the names of the people who live three houses down from us at home. In Lexington, we sort of belong to a bunch of separate communities. Like, the members of my basketball team make up one; the girls in choir, another. But here, each place is a community, it seems. A community of people from valley to valley or mountain to mountain.

I could hardly believe that an eighty-five-year-old woman doctor would drive her car all the way up to Grandpa Mosley's place, then walk up the hill, to look at Grandmommy's toe. Dr. Grace was so bent over that she had to lift her head to look you in the face. She seemed to know what she was doing, though, and I don't think she thought much of Mammaw's homemade salve, made of whiskey and turpentine and I-don't-know-what-all.

This probably sounds like I'm starting to judge them already, and I hope I'm not. But I'm beginning to see ways we're different. I have to be honest. Hygiene doesn't seem as important to them, though just washing up is more complicated than you'd think. But Megan told me that Ivy June's family probably keeps an old catalog in their

180

outhouse and uses the pages for toilet paper, and fortunately that's not true.

I'm more tired here than I am at home. Everything we do takes more energy. The long walk to catch the bus—that kind of thing. Ivy June's grandfather goes to bed when the sun goes down, and he leaves before Ivy June and I get up.

At least the weather's been warm, and that's a help. "Warmest March on record," Grandpa Mosley said last night at the supper table. He can hardly wait to start their garden.

I can hardly wait to wash my hair.

Catherine Combs

CHAPTER THIRTY

April 1

Catherine _would_ have to be here on April first.
You'd think it was a national holiday the way
the fool boys at school carry on—seventh graders
acting like a bunch of kids in elementary.

On the bus, Perry Lewis taped something on the
back of Dennis Reed, and when everyone got
off, kids started kicking Dennis because he was
wearing a sign that read KICK ME HARD. You
don't dare sit down anywhere in school on April
Fool's Day without checking the seat for
thumbtacks, and I had to watch out for Catherine
the whole day. But I didn't watch close enough,
because one of the girls at our table—I don't know

who—stuck a flat rubber spider under Catherine's milk carton. When she picked it up and saw the spider, she gave a shriek and scooted away—milk all over the place.

Everyone laughed then, and Catherine turned that funny shade of pink. But she laughed too, and I helped her wipe up the milk. I was sure glad when we got off the bus this afternoon. I don't think it was Shirl who put the spider there, but I wouldn't bet on it. She hasn't said anything against Catherine so far, but she hasn't said anything for her either.

I kept my eyes on Howard every step of the way home when I found him waiting for us at the bus stop. I told him yesterday he didn't have to wait for us after school, I know the way home, but there he was. Catherine asked him what he liked best about living in the mountains, and he just shrugged. "Howard, you got a bone stuck in your throat?" I asked him.

All he did was smile and kick a stone, then kick it again, but finally he said, "I don't know. Never lived anywhere else."

That's fair enough, I guess. How's he supposed to know what he likes best if he doesn't have anything to compare it with? That's why I was sent to Lexington, I guess. To see what's different.

I thought maybe he was getting a crush on

Catherine, because he didn't stay at Ma's after we crossed the creek. Just followed us up to Mammaw's, ate her ginger cookies, and took off. It was a half hour later when Catherine went to the outhouse that we heard the scream. Howard had dragged that caged raccoon to the side of the outhouse and watched for Catherine to make a visit. Soon as he saw her coming, he must have shoved that creature inside, and Catherine found it. How he trapped the fool thing in the first place or got it in the outhouse, I don't know. But if it had been me found that animal, I would have held Howard by the heels and dropped him in the hole myself, I was that mad.

I went charging back into the kitchen, where he was laughing up a storm, and soon as I told Mammaw what he'd done, she reached for Papaw's razor strop, but Howard was out of there and halfway down the hill before she could catch him, just whooping it up.

"That boy gets the prize for foolishness," Mammaw said.

When Catherine's heartbeat had returned to normal, she was still as polite as ever. "Brothers like to kid around," she said, as though Peter pulled tricks like that on her all the time. I was about to ask if she ever got mad at anybody for anything, and then I remembered the time she was mad at me and let it go.

That night I asked if she'd been able to reach anyone on her cell phone. She said no, which means she tried. I just hope she wasn't trying to call home and ask somebody to come pick her up. Wouldn't blame her if she did.

Ivy June Mosley

CHAPTER THIRTY-ONE

When Ivy June and Catherine stopped by Ma's house on the way back from school on Wednesday, Ruth Mosley was clearly upset. Daddy's truck was gone, but he was there—out on the back stoop smoking a cigarette, strictly against doctor's orders.

"What's wrong?" Ivy June asked.

"Russell's truck broke down over near Cutshin," her mother said. "The Prathers had to bring him home. And he'd just hired on to help build their extra room."

"Can't the pickup be fixed?"

"Transmission and I-don't-know-what-all," Mrs. Mosley said, one hand nervously stroking her throat. "First off it has to be towed somewhere a man can fix it, but Mr. Prather himself poked around and says it don't look good."

Ivy June didn't have to be told just how bad this was.

Not only was there the cost of repairs to consider, but also the fact that Daddy now had no way to get back and forth to work at Cutshin. He'd been told that the job would probably last two or three weeks, and he couldn't afford to lose that income. Ma answered the question Ivy June didn't ask:

"Ed Prather's going to hire somebody else. Says he's sorry, but he can't drive fifty miles each mornin' to pick Russell up and bring him back. And them with a new baby on the way, they need that extra room bad."

Solutions swirled around in Ivy June's head and were just as quickly rejected. Papaw couldn't drive Daddy to work because he'd have his car at the mine. Jessie couldn't do it; she'd need her car to get to the factory. Those were steady jobs they had to keep. Daddy only worked part-time at whatever he could find, and when Papaw retired, his pension would have to provide for them all.

Catherine stood by silently, concerned.

"I'm really sorry, and I can see he is too," Ivy June said, watching her daddy through the window.

Mrs. Mosley let out her breath, and her hand dropped to her side. "Just can't never get ahead, it seems. Take one step forward and you get two steps back. There goes that new refrigerator I wanted. Don't look now like I'll ever get it."

On the way up the hill to Mammaw's, Catherine said, "Since your dad's health isn't so good and . . . now this . . . why wouldn't you . . . you know . . . apply for welfare? I mean, it's not as though he's not trying."

"Papaw wouldn't stand for it!" Ivy June said emphatically. "He says as long as he's alive, there won't be one Mosley on the giveaway. But if it weren't for Papaw and his paycheck, and the little that Jessie makes, I don't know what we'd do."

She wondered why she was telling Catherine this—Catherine, of all people. Catherine, with the gold locket around her neck and the big house back in Lexington. But the weariness in Ma's voice and the slump of Daddy's shoulders out on the stoop made the situation too obvious to cover up. She went on: "Papaw still talks about the big sturdy man he saw up in Hazard in the supermart, paying for a cart full of groceries with food stamps. 'Why, I'd be ashamed,' he said. He thinks every able-bodied man ought to work."

"Well . . . your dad would if he could," said Catherine.

"I know. Ma says we're born back here in the hollow, where there aren't any jobs, and to get to where there's work, you need a car. But you can't buy a car if you don't have the money. And you don't have the money if you don't work. People say, 'Well, why don't you move to where the jobs are?' But what house do we move to, and how do we pay for getting there? That's what Ma wants to know."

Ivy June was suddenly embarrassed by her outburst, and pressed her lips together to keep from saying more.

"No simple answers, I guess," said Catherine.

"Not simple at all," said Ivy June.

Mammaw took the news about the pickup truck grimly. "Well," she said, "there's number two." She silently shook her head, then pointed to the willow basket by the door. "Bring in the dry clothes, will you, girls?"

Out on the porch, as they checked to see which of the hanging clothes were still damp, Catherine asked, "What did she mean by that?"

"She's wondering what will happen next," said Ivy June. "Trouble comes in threes, she says, and Grandmommy's infected foot was number one."

"So you go around expecting something awful to happen?" Catherine asked, astonished.

"Sooner or later, it does," said Ivy June.

"Well, sooner or later, good things happen too," said Catherine. "That doesn't prove anything."

"I could count on one hand the number of good things that just might happen out of the blue," Ivy June said, a slight edge to her voice.

"You got to be in the exchange program, didn't you?" Catherine said, but when Ivy June didn't answer, she quickly changed the subject. "Anyway, who was that boy who said hi to you in the cafeteria?"

Ivy June dropped a clothespin into the cloth bag at the end of the porch. "Just somebody," she said. And then, mimicking Catherine, "*Not* my boyfriend."

Catherine laughed. "Okay. But does he have a name?"

"Jimmy Harris. And that's all there is to tell."

"Except how cute he is."

"*You* said it, not me," said Ivy June, and grinned.

⟨⟨⟨

Ivy June had promised Catherine that they could wash their hair that weekend, but by Thursday morning, Catherine was so upset over her stringy hair that she rummaged through her suitcase for a springy metal headband she wore sometimes. Combing back her hair, she placed the blue headband over the top of her head, the ends coming down behind her ears. It gave her a sleek look and kept her long hair from hanging down the sides of her face.

"This is my trick when I'm having a bad hair day," she said. And then, sensing Ivy June's interest in it, she said, "I've got an extra. Do you want it?"

She dug around some more for the red band, and Ivy June tried it on. She was pleased with how it looked.

"It's pretty," Ivy June said.

She forgot about it after they set off for the bus stop, because as they walked, they asked each other questions to prepare for their history quiz. What were the causes of World War II? Which was the first country to surrender? What was the Marshall Plan? The questions were more difficult for Catherine because her class back at the Academy hadn't done the world wars yet.

When the girls got on the bus, Ivy June automatically looked around for Shirl and found her sitting in the back row again with the boys. One of them, sitting next to the boy beside her, kept reaching around the fellow's back and tickling Shirl's neck, and, not knowing who did it, Shirl was happily swatting at each boy in turn as they all took part in the teasing.

When Shirley saw Ivy June and Catherine, however, she paused. "Well, well, looks like we got twins today," she said, pointing to her head. "Bet even their underwear matches." The boys guffawed.

Ivy June stared at her. "Shirl . . . ?" she said.

But Shirley turned away and invited more tickles from the boys.

Ivy June slid quietly onto a seat, and Catherine sat down next to her. Was Shirl jealous? Because of a headband? Forty minutes later, when the bus stopped at the entrance to the school, Catherine moved with the others toward the front of the bus, but Ivy June waited for Shirl so she could walk with her. Shirl, though, was laughing and hanging on to one of the boys as she passed, and pointedly ignored Ivy June.

"Shirl . . . ," Ivy June called again when she stepped off the bus behind them. But with a toss of her head, Shirl walked through the door with the boys and on down the hall to her locker.

⁂

It was warm—so warm that kids were taking off their jackets and eating their lunches outside. The feathery lavender of new growth on the tips of branches was more distinct now, and the white snowdrop flowers on the south side of the building had been replaced by the bright yellow of daffodils. Ivy June looked around for Shirl, but she must have stayed indoors.

Jimmy Harris came over to the bench where Ivy June and Catherine were sitting.

"Got anything in that lunch sack for me?" he asked, grinning, as Ivy June popped a piece of oatmeal cookie in her mouth.

"That all you think about? Your stomach?" Ivy June asked, and handed him her second cookie, which he accepted.

"No. Think about you sometimes," he said, the smile even wider on his face.

"Yeah, right," said Ivy June, but she was pleased, and it showed. "This is Catherine Combs, case you haven't met. Visiting us for two weeks."

"How you doin'?" said Jimmy, and turned back to Ivy June. "Well, what I wanted to know was, are you going to Earl's tomorrow? Supposed to be a nice night."

Ivy June looked at Catherine. "You want to go if Jessie will drive us?"

"Sure!" said Catherine. "I guess so."

"Well, maybe I'll see you there if my sister will take us," Ivy June said.

"Tell her I'll even get Earl to come out and dance with her if she will," said Jimmy, and Ivy June laughed.

"Wait till you get a load of Earl," she said to Catherine.

She looked around again for Shirl, but her friend was definitely avoiding her. Too bad, because Shirl would have been the first one Ivy June told about Jimmy Harris.

When the girls got off the bus that afternoon, Howard was nowhere to be seen. He'd been making himself scarce since the raccoon incident, and as Catherine and Ivy June walked the mile back to Mammaw's, Ivy June asked, "Want to see my favorite place?"

"What kind of place?"

"Where I go when I want to be by myself."

"All right," Catherine agreed. "But you won't be by yourself."

"I'll pretend you're not there," Ivy June said with a smile.

They went across the porch and into the kitchen, where Mammaw was making dried-apple pies. A short stack of half-moon pastries sat to one side of her floured board, waiting for the oven. Deftly, she traced circles around a plate on the rolled-out dough, dropped a scoop of dried apples and sugar on one half of each circle, then flopped the other half over and pressed the edges together with her thumb.

"Ummm. Looks good," said Catherine.

Mammaw smiled. "Figured we needed a little something extra to cheer us up," she said.

"We're going up the mountain," Ivy June told her grandmother.

"Take a couple cookies for your pocket," Mammaw said. "And there's some old apples in the box out there— need to be eaten up."

As they climbed the steep path, grabbing at tree roots, Ivy June said, "This is about my most favorite place in the whole world."

"Right here?"

"No, on up a way."

"Can't imagine many other people trying to find it," said Catherine, panting a little. "I'm trying not to look behind me."

"Don't worry. If you fell, the thornbushes would stop you," Ivy June said. "We're almost there."

They reached the ridge halfway from the top, where the three small saplings grew side by side a few feet from the edge of the cliff, a mossy bed beneath them.

"Here," said Ivy June, and sank down on the moss. Catherine gratefully joined her.

"I call it the Whistling Place," Ivy June explained, "because when the wind blows, it makes a whistling sound. You can hear it best when the trees leaf out."

Catherine listened. "I don't hear anything."

"It's not going to whistle just for you. Wait for a breeze," Ivy June told her.

Catherine clasped her knees and slowly turned her head from left to right. "Wow!" she said. "I think I see your house down there. And there's the little bridge. Look how Thunder Creek winds around!"

Ivy June pointed out the trail to Vulture's Pass, and the hill they used for sledding in the winter.

"It's all so beautiful," said Catherine. "Do you ever come here with Jimmy Harris?"

Ivy June gave her leg a poke. "Of course not." Then she added, "When I come up here, it's like everything starts out new. You want to sing something? Sometimes I come up here and sing."

"What song?" asked Catherine.

Ivy June thought for a moment. Then she lifted her head and sang out clear and steady: "*Annie, Annie . . .*"

And as soon as she started "*. . . was the miller's daughter,*" Catherine joined in:

"*Annie, Annie . . .*" Her singing was a little shaky at first, but then she sang louder, more sure of herself. "*. . . was the miller's daughter; far she wandered, by the singing water . . .*"

When Ivy June finished singing it the first time, she began all over again, and their voices seemed to echo against the rock walls of the mountain: "*. . . by the singing water . . .*"

After the third time, Ivy June slowed on the last few words: "*. . . bring your white sheep home,*" and Catherine's voice trailed after: "*. . . bring . . . your . . . white . . . sheep . . . home.*"

Struck by the beauty of it, they sat for a moment, as though the echo was yet to come, pleased at the sounds they had made.

And then, from somewhere below them, "*Annie, Annie, wah wah wah wah wah wah.*"

The girls jerked around.

"Howard!" Ivy June yelled, springing to her feet.

But with a whoop and a bellow, Howard was already

195

scrambling back down the path, slipping and sliding, laughing himself sick.

〰

After Papaw came home from the mine on Friday, the family ate an early supper so that he could get to bed about eight. He had to work on Saturday this week, so he would be going off before dawn one more morning before he could rest. Ivy June and Catherine waited until they were sure he was in bed before they prepared for their baths and hair-washing out on the enclosed back porch.

"Be sure Howard doesn't walk in on us," Ivy June said to Mammaw.

"I don't think Howard's going to show himself any time soon, the way you girls were chasin' and screechin' at him yesterday. Got all the dogs to howlin' clear up to Vulture's Pass."

"Well, he'd better *not* show up, because I'm going to punch him good when he does," Ivy June declared.

The girls took their soap and shampoo and towels out to the big tin washtub and made sure that Mammaw's flowered curtains were pulled over every square inch of window. They pumped cold water from the porch pump until it was four inches deep in the washtub, then added the large pail of hot water Mammaw had left on the bench. When Ivy June came back into the kitchen for the teakettle, Mammaw said, "Land sakes, Ivy June, add some cold to the kettle before you pour it over yourselves. Water's always hotter on your head than it is on your hand."

Ivy June did, and checked the temperature with one finger before she took it back out and closed the door. Catherine had already slipped off her clothes and was clutching a towel around her body. She looked about uneasily before stepping, giggling, into the tub, letting the towel drop at the last possible second. When she sat down, knees scrunched up to her chin, the water came within an inch of the top.

Ivy June slowly poured a bit of water from the kettle over Catherine's head. Catherine shivered, then quickly added shampoo and began to scrub. "Oh, man, this feels good," she said.

"Well, scratch away," said Ivy June. "Mammaw's got another kettle ready if we need it."

Catherine's teeth chattered as soap suds rose on her head and water trickled down her body. "I'm already freezing," she said. "How do you ever wash yourselves in winter?"

"We bring the tub into the kitchen in front of the stove," said Ivy June. "If Papaw didn't have ten people to support, two houses, two cars, and a broken-down truck, he'd have his indoor bathroom by now. That's what Mammaw wants more than anything."

"What about your friends?"

"Some of them have bathrooms. It's us up here in the hollows who are waaaaay behind on that."

Catherine scrubbed a little more. "Rinse time!" she said finally, and Ivy June reached again for the kettle.

When Catherine was through at last, she wrapped herself in the towel as she stood up and she and Ivy June traded places.

"You're bathing in my dirty water?" Catherine asked, horrified.

"Not *that* dirty," Ivy June replied. "You want to heat some more water and empty this tub out the door, it's okay with me."

Catherine reconsidered. "Well, I don't care if you don't," she said.

Afterward, when they were dressed, Catherine stood in front of the small mirror in Ivy June's bedroom, blow-dryer plugged into the one electric outlet. Her hair dryer and shampoos and conditioners had almost filled one of the smaller bags she'd brought with her. She used a stiff-bristled brush to roll up the ends of her hair, laboriously drying each lock. Ivy June watched enviously as the curls fell loosely around Catherine's shoulders.

Catherine caught her expression. "Want me to do yours?"

Ivy June thought of Shirl—the way she had reacted to the matching headbands. But then, thinking of Jimmy Harris, she said, "Curl away," and stood patiently while Catherine worked the brush and the blow-dryer.

༄

Shirl was at Earl's store, and so was Fred Mason. Ivy June saw them at the far end of the parking lot. They were dancing as close as the slices of bread in a grilled cheese sandwich. Howard had not been allowed to come—his punishment for teasing the girls—so Ivy June and Catherine had ridden alone with Jessie. Ivy June noticed that her sister had traded her sweatshirt for a sweater and put on eyeliner.

"You going to come back for us at ten?" she asked as they got out of the car at the edge of the parking area.

"Oh, I'll be around," Jessie said casually, and Ivy June was pleased to see her park the car down the road and walk back to where a dozen or so couples were dancing on the asphalt.

Older couples, Ma and Daddy's age, sat together on Earl's steps or in the rockers up on the long porch. But there were a few couples in their twenties—several more hanging around the edges of the crowd—and they had come a bit more dressed up, the girls in slick-soled shoes, not sneakers. Earl himself—a big man in a plaid shirt and suspenders—called out to ask if the music was loud enough, then turned the volume up even more. The first song ended and a second, a number called "Blue Rockabilly," blared through the speakers at either end of the porch.

Laughing self-consciously, Ivy June and Catherine faced each other and began to dance, mimicking each other's foot swivels and finger snapping, exaggerating the movements of their hips to make each other laugh.

When they felt a little bolder, they moved into the more brightly lighted half of the parking lot while couples edged into the shadows. Ivy June nudged Catherine when

199

she saw Jessie dancing with a young man who looked as new at it as Jessie was.

Jimmy Harris was there, standing over at the side of the porch with the other boys, horsing around. Ivy June was sure he had seen her, but he didn't seem to be paying attention. Like a lot of boys, she thought, he was shy with girls around his friends. But later that evening, he and a buddy came over and began a crazy kind of dancing that made Ivy June and Catherine smile.

"You want something to drink?" Jimmy asked when there was a break in the music. Earl was selling cans of Coke and Mountain Dew chilled in a tub of ice. "Thanks," said Ivy June. "I'll take a Coke."

His buddy bought one for Catherine.

They sat on tree stumps serving as a fence at one end of the parking lot. Jimmy's buddy was trying to do a trick with his Mountain Dew can, balancing it on the end of one finger, but it spilled all over his jeans, and Jimmy hooted at him. The boy laughed too, and took off his shirt to wipe his jeans, showing a fine, broad chest that made Catherine smile and turn away.

Fred Mason had his arm around Shirl and was trying to maneuver her back behind Earl's store. She was giggling and turning him around toward the parking lot, and when she saw Ivy June and Catherine sitting side by side on the tree stumps, she guided him over.

Stepping right in front of Ivy June, Shirl studied the long blond hair, shiny under the high-intensity bulbs of the lot, the curls at the ends, and then at Catherine's dark hair, curled the same way.

"That the new hairstyle up in Lexington?" she asked with a laugh and, pulling Fred Mason around in a circle, danced back across the lot.

◊◊◊

When Ivy June opened her eyes the next morning, she wasn't sure if it was Saturday or Sunday. She didn't hear Papaw moving around in the kitchen making flapjacks the way he did on weekends, but it couldn't be a school morning because it was already light outside.

Then she remembered that Papaw was working six days this week. It was Saturday, and there was nowhere she had to go, so she snuggled down under the blanket and let her mind play out scenes from the night before: she and Catherine doing the new duck dance, everybody waddling around and laughing; Jimmy Harris's buddy spilling Mountain Dew on his jeans; and—she'd saved the best till last—Jimmy holding her hand as he walked her back to Jessie's car after the dancing was over. Jessie had had a good time too, talking to Earl's cousin up there on the porch. Then Ivy June remembered Shirl's remark about her hair. She frowned to herself and rolled over.

Catherine's bed was empty, so Ivy June got up and slipped out the back way, passing Catherine coming back from the outhouse.

"Your grandmother says we can have breakfast in our pajamas on the front porch," Catherine told her.

"The *porch?*" exclaimed Ivy June.

"She's got Grandmommy out there. Says it's turning colder this afternoon, so we should enjoy the weather while we can."

It *was* a beautiful morning, Ivy June decided. The kind of morning that if she were on a ranch in Oklahoma, or a stage in Lexington, she'd be sitting on a fence singing "Oh, What a Beautiful Mornin'."

Mammaw had placed a platter of scrambled eggs and bacon on a small wooden table just outside the front door. There was also some of her fried toast, thick slices of buttered bread grilled on top of the iron stove. Papaw had told her long ago that they could afford an electric one, but Mammaw wouldn't have it. Said she'd have to learn to cook a whole new way, that she'd take a new washing machine before she got a new stove.

Grandmommy was enjoying the sun. She had her feet on a stool, sticking right out where the sun could reach them, and her toothless mouth worked itself up and down as she rubbed her thin fingers together and turned her head to the right or left when she heard a crow's call or the distant bark of a dog. It seemed to Ivy June that the worse her vision got, the more her hearing improved.

"This is heaven!" said Catherine, reaching for another slice of warm bread and slathering it with Mammaw's wild strawberry jam. "Mom loved those preserves you gave us," she told Mammaw. "We already finished one jar and started the second."

"Then I'll send a jar or two back home with you," said Mammaw, pleased. "I got just enough to last us till berry season comes again." She leaned forward and checked the sky. "See the clouds? That'll tell you the cold's coming in, but I don't feel it yet." She turned to Grandmommy. "You all right there, Iree?"

"I'm okay," said the old woman. "But it's the last spring."

Ivy June and Catherine stopped chewing and looked at Grandmommy.

"Now, Iree, why do you think that?" Mammaw asked her. "When a woman lives to be a hundred, why . . . no telling *how* much longer she could live!"

"Last spring for *some*body," Grandmommy said, and her fingers curled and uncurled again, resting on the faded dress.

Mammaw pondered that awhile, leaning back in the rocker and letting the breeze fan her face. "Well, it's always the last spring for somebody, Iree, but it don't have to be you," she said. And turning to the girls, "You have a good time down at Earl's last night? Myrtle Tolson tells me that on Friday and Saturday nights, the cars is parked every which way on the road outside Earl's. She says one night there was even a license plate from Virginia. We get people coming in here from across the mountain, why, who knows what could happen."

"Maybe it was just somebody visiting relatives," said Ivy June, smiling a little.

"Well, if Earl's gets any more popular, and then that barbecue place catches on . . ."·

Mammaw stopped talking suddenly and leaned forward again, staring off down the hill. Ivy June and Catherine turned to see what had caught her attention.

Something was coming their way, bobbing slowly up and down, and at first Ivy June thought it was a man holding a boy on his shoulders. Then, squinting, she realized it was a man on horseback, coming up the hill from the footbridge.

"Trouble comes in threes," rasped Mammaw, unblinking, her hands tightening their hold on the arms of the rocker.

Ivy June felt her own hands grow cold and her heart began to pound as Sam Feeley, the man with the ham radio, rode into the yard.

CHAPTER THIRTY-TWO

The short, muscular man dismounted and tied the reins of his horse loosely around a dogwood at one side of the yard.

"I knew it! I knew it!" whispered Mammaw.

"Hello there, Emma," Mr. Feeley called, with a slight tip of his cap. "Hello, Iree."

Grandmommy's head swiveled in the direction of the voice, but Mammaw didn't return the greeting. Her body stiff, she said, "Sam, what you got to tell us?"

Papaw! Ivy June's breath was coming out fast and shaky. Five more hours and his shift at the mine would have ended.

"State police radioed me this morning to take a message here, seeing as how I'm a little closer . . . ," Mr. Feeley said.

Ivy June stared at him, wondering if she'd been glad to see him, ever, always thinking of Mr. Feeley as a person full of bad news.

"You got a girl staying here named Catherine?" the man asked.

Ivy June blinked. Mammaw looked about in confusion. "Why, yes, this here is Catherine. She's from Lexington."

Sam Feeley touched the rim of his cap again as he turned toward Catherine. He wore a flannel shirt of brown and yellow plaid, and his belt buckle was hidden entirely by his large stomach, despite his small frame.

Mr. Feeley pulled a piece of paper from one shirt pocket, his glasses from the other. "Seems your father tried to get a message to the school, but it's closed, of course, and he couldn't reach a teacher. . . . Julia Dixon? That the name? So he called the state police and left a message, and I scribbled down what they told me best I could."

"What's *happened?*" asked Catherine.

"Says your mom fainted on . . . Thursday, I guess it was . . . and that they've discovered her . . . weakness, is it? . . . isn't because of the pneumonia, but a heart condition. Your dad's taking her to the Cleveland Clinic. . . ." Mr. Feeley adjusted his glasses. "Yes, that's it. Cleveland Clinic. And she's going to have an operation."

Catherine gave a little cry, and Mammaw reached over from the rocker and clasped her arm.

206

"Now, your dad says for you not to worry, that she's got the best of doctors, and for you not to come home," Mr. Feeley went on. "He says he wants you to stay right here like you planned. . . . Let's see now. . . . Oh, yes. Peter and Claire are staying with Gramps and Rose . . . Rosemary, and there's nothing you could do by coming home."

Sam Feeley took off his glasses and stuck them back in his pocket. "I'd let you read this yourself, but you'd never make out my handwritin'. Can hardly read it myself. Sure sorry about your mother, but it sounds like they're doing the right thing."

"But . . . what kind of operation, and when is it going to be? Why did they have to go to Cleveland?" Catherine asked. Her eyes grew moist and the corners of her mouth sagged. "How long will they be there?"

Mammaw squeezed her arm. "Honey, your daddy couldn't tell you what he don't know yet himself."

"But I have to talk to my mother!" Catherine said, the tears spilling over. "I should *be* there!"

"I'm sorry, miss," Sam Feeley said again, "but seems to me if your dad thought you ought to be there, he'd've sent for you, and someone would drive you back. Best to do just like he says." He turned to Mammaw again. "Sure hate to be the one bringing bad news. Many a time I've wished I didn't have that old radio."

"Last spring for somebody," murmured Grandmommy, her fingers twitching, and Catherine jumped up and ran inside.

Ivy June started to follow, but Mammaw stopped her. "Let her cry alone a little, Ivy June. Then you go to her," she said.

"Wasn't sure just how the road was up this way," Sam continued. "Week before last, the road from Pippa Passes to Pine Top was so muddy I couldn't drive through. Didn't know how it'd be over thisaway. Figured old Brandy here could bring me over maybe better'n my car."

"Got some cider, Sam. Turning a little hard, but it's cold," Mammaw said. "Won't you set down and have a glass? Piece of pound cake?"

"Might take that cider," the stocky man said, sitting down on the chair Catherine had left. "Sure sorry about the news. Not the kind of thing you want to hear when you're away from home."

Ivy June got up then and went inside. Walked quickly through the parlor and into the tiny room where Catherine was sprawled on the bed, sobbing, one pajama leg twisted around her knee.

Ivy June crawled onto the cot and over to the single bed next to it. "Cat," she said softly, "it's going to be all right."

"You don't know that!" Catherine cried all the harder.

"She's got the best doctors, your dad said! If he thought something bad would happen, he'd have asked us to drive you home."

"That's not it! They just want to protect me. They never tell me anything serious!" Catherine wept, her nose sounding clogged. "After Grandma died, I didn't even know Gramps knew a woman named Rosemary. And the next thing I find out, he's getting married. It's always worse when they don't tell you and you find out later. I want to *be* with my mom! I want to hug her!"

Ivy June looked around desperately, then reached out and picked up the gold locket from the backless chair that served as her bedside table. "Hold on to this, Cat," she said. "It'll be like touching your mom, with her picture inside."

Catherine raised her head and stared at the locket through her tears. "It will not! That's stupid, like you and your rock! That's not going to help!"

Her throat tight, Ivy June put the locket back on the chair. She sat motionless on the cot, staring at her feet. They looked awkward, somehow—too big for her legs compared to Catherine's size six-and-a-halfs. Her pajamas, thin with wear, looked faded beside the bright little pink and red hearts on Catherine's.

But Catherine wasn't through yet. She bolted up suddenly and leaned back against the wall, her face red and puffy and wet, her nose clogged: "I know you're trying to be helpful, Ivy June, but you're not! Your grandmother saying all the time she knew something bad was going to happen! She did not! Nobody knew this, not even Dad! We all thought it was pneumonia."

"You're right," said Ivy June. "Mammaw didn't know."

They could hear Sam Feeley saying his goodbyes out

on the porch, then the soft clop of the horse's hooves on the bare ground, fading off into the distance.

Ivy June rolled off the cot. "Let's go up to the Whispering Place," she said. "Let's put on our jeans and just climb."

For a moment Catherine didn't respond. Then, wordlessly, she got off the bed, picked up her clothes, and dressed.

"We're going up the mountain," Ivy June said to Mammaw as they went out and crossed the porch. Mammaw nodded.

There was a cool feel to the air now. The clouds were moving faster overhead, and when the girls reached the high ridge, the wind whistled through the saplings and Catherine stopped, listening, before she sat down.

For a long time neither girl spoke, just sat tuned to the wind's whisperings, watching shadows scoot across the valley floor.

"If she dies," Catherine said at last, "I won't have had the chance to tell her I love her."

Ivy June studied her friend's face. "Haven't you shown her in a hundred ways already?" she asked.

"It's not the same as saying it," said Catherine, and her voice sounded tense, controlled. "I just need to be with . . . with my family. With Gramps. Even Rosemary. Well, not Rosemary, maybe. But people who know that these things can happen. It's *not* trouble number three, like it *had* to come. It *doesn't* prove that superstition. And if Mom . . . dies, it doesn't have anything to do with a hundred-year-old woman saying that it's somebody's last spring."

There was anger in Catherine's words. In her eyes. She seemed to be glaring at Ivy June, but then she turned and looked again out over the valley.

"Well, I never said *I* believed that," Ivy June said defensively.

"Maybe not, but I'll bet you thought it. Just because your grandmother and great-grandmother and all the grandmothers before them believe something doesn't make it true. No matter how many grandmothers put whiskey and turpentine on infections, that doesn't mean it cures. You shouldn't *do* things or *believe* things just because everybody who lived before you did."

She set her jaw and gave Ivy June the same look as before. This time Ivy June glared back, anger roiling inside her. Never mind how upset Catherine might be, Ivy June wouldn't let her go after Mammaw.

"Well, *we're* not the ones who go to a private school just because our mother did. We're not the ones who go into the printing business just because it belonged to our daddy." Ivy June's voice was shaking as she delivered that last line.

Catherine looked at her wide-eyed. "There's a difference between wanting to keep a company going and keeping a superstition going," she snapped.

"Even if your dad really wanted to be a pilot?" Ivy

June shot back. "Down here the mine's about all we've got. But in Lexington, your daddy could have been anything he wanted."

Catherine blanched. "At least *our* traditions make sense."

"A little boy having to wear a *tie* makes sense? Just because he's going to the theater? That's as silly as . . ." Ivy June stopped. What was *happening* here? What were they *saying*? "Let's just both of us shut up and listen to the wind," she said.

For a long time they did.

At last Catherine took a deep breath, her shoulders rising with resolution, then falling again. "I'm going to pretend we didn't say any of this," she told Ivy June.

"We can pretend, but it happened. No use playing like it didn't."

"But it's so . . . so prejudiced!" said Catherine. "I was just upset about Mom."

"And I'm sorry about your ma," said Ivy June. "I'd want to be back home too if I were you."

"We're still friends, aren't we?" Catherine asked. "I'd hate staying here if you were mad at me."

Ivy June knew exactly how that felt. "Of course we're friends," she said.

◊◊◊

They went back to the house, and Mammaw got out her scrap basket, filled with the small pieces of cloth she had saved from sewing projects, declaring she needed a new rag rug for just inside the door.

"It's hard to keep your mind on two things at once," she said to the girls, "and if your hands are busy, you may not fret so much over what you can't do one single thing about." She poked around through the ten-inch strips, all cut the same length, and selected a blue one and a yellow print. There were strips from old curtains, too, and from chair covers and bedspreads.

"What I want you to do," she said, "is tie the ends of these pieces together into three long strips, all the same length. Like this." Her knobby fingers demonstrated. "Then, when the scraps are all used up, we'll braid the three long strips together, pulled nice and tight, till we've got us one long cloth rope. After that I'll coil it around and around itself and stitch it all together. Looks good, don't you think? Got me some fine colors there."

Ivy June couldn't tell if Catherine wanted the job or not, but she was too polite, as always, to refuse. And somehow it did seem to help. Mammaw turned the radio on to a country music station, one of only two stations they could get here in the hollow, and as Catherine's fingers sorted through the basket, looking for colors that looked nice together, she relaxed a little and even smiled once or twice.

"Catherine," Papaw said when he came home and heard the news about her mother, "when someone's in a worrying place, it's a comfort to know the family is carrying on, same as before. Your ma's right where she should be now, and you carrying on as she planned is what she needs to hear. The minute your daddy wants you someplace else, we'll take you there. Is that something you can hold on to?"

"I . . . I guess," said Catherine.

About five, Ezra came running up the hill to say that Miss Dixon was down at the house and wanted to tell Catherine some more about her mother. Catherine dropped her work and flew out the door, Ivy June following close behind. Breathless, they ran down the hill and up the steps to Ma's house, where the teacher was sitting on the swing, Ma on a folding chair across from her, Danny on Ma's lap. Howard, who stood at the side of the house, seemed ready to run at the slightest scowl from Ivy June.

Miss Dixon got up and hugged Catherine, then pulled her down on the swing beside her. "When I came back from shopping this morning, there was a message from your dad that he'd tried to reach me, and he left a number for me to call. I did—his cell phone, I think—and he said that your mother was admitted to the Cleveland Clinic and was resting comfortably. Your doctor in Lexington had recommended a heart specialist there and made the arrangements."

"How bad is it?" Catherine asked.

"I don't know the details, Catherine, but the surgery is scheduled for Monday morning. Your dad said he would call you at school as soon as it's over. We'll let you take the call in the office. He said to tell you that your mom knows how much you want to be there, but she feels much better knowing that you're here with Ivy June. Peter and Claire are doing fine at your grandparents'."

Catherine tipped back her head and closed her eyes. When she opened them again, she said, "I think that not knowing—not being there—is the worst of all."

"That's the truth," said Mrs. Mosley. "I remember one evening I near worried myself to death when Russell was out in a snowstorm. He never did get back the whole night, and I imagined him froze somewhere out on the road. All the while a neighbor had taken him in, and he was warm and toasty as could be. But there was no way of me knowing that. I'd have a hundred times wished myself out in that snowstorm dealing with it than sitting here worrying about what *might* be."

"Well, I promised your father that if he had any more messages for you, I'd drive up here just as soon as I could and deliver them," Miss Dixon said to Catherine. "I just didn't want you to worry all weekend."

"Thank you," Catherine said, and smiled a little when Danny slid off his mother's lap and came over to hug Catherine's legs in sympathy.

As the girls went back up the hill later, Catherine said, "Please don't tell anyone at school about Mom, okay?"

"What's so shameful about being sick?" Ivy June asked.

"I don't want people asking about her when I don't have any answers yet. I don't want them treating me any different because of her."

"All right," Ivy June agreed.

〰️

There was chicken for dinner that evening, with noodles that Mammaw had made by hand. Ivy June fed Grandmommy at the table, mashing green beans into mush, and keeping a dish towel tucked in the neck of the old woman's dress to catch the spills.

Mammaw dished up the applesauce and the green beans she had canned the summer before. She took a fresh pan of biscuits out of the oven and served the stewed tomatoes and okra, all the time telling about a squirrel that had got in the crawl space under the roof once, and the trouble Papaw had trying to get it out. Catherine listened, eating sparingly, but at least she ate.

Later, Catherine and Ivy June washed themselves at the kitchen sink and put on their pajamas in front of the woodstove. The rain that had begun around dinnertime came down heavier now, and the house creaked as the wind picked up. After they got into bed, Ivy June noticed that Catherine reached for her mother's locket on the backless chair and, enclosing it tightly in one hand, put her head on the pillow.

CHAPTER THIRTY-THREE

April 6

House is still as a morgue, except for
Grandmommy's whining. She's all confused about
who went to Cleveland and "where that new girl's
off to now." If she says "last spring for somebody"
one more time, I'll scream. Catherine will, anyway.

We didn't go to church with Papaw and
Mammaw; Catherine didn't want to, and Mammaw
didn't insist. So I went down to the house and told
Jessie she didn't have to sit with Grandmommy, I'd
do it. Daddy's out smoking again. Ma says he's
going to drive Jessie's car to the man in Cutshin
this afternoon, see if he thinks the truck is worth
fixing up or does Daddy have to buy another one.

I came back to Mammaw's to eat my breakfast. Catherine stayed in the bedroom doing her math problems. It's so quiet you can hear the skitter of a squirrel on a limb near the outhouse.

When Mammaw got back from church, she made an A   Sunday dinner. This time we had ham with the fried chicken, potatoes with giblet gravy, boiled eggs pickled in beet juice, and biscuits with rhubarb preserves.

Papaw folded his hands at the table and said, "We pray the Lord that he look down on Catherine's mother in Cleveland, and that the doctors feel his presence in the operating room. We ask that she be blessed with health, so that she can be a testament to the Lord's handiwork. Amen."

That set Grandmommy off again, asking about Cleveland, but one bite of Mammaw's biscuits, she got her mind on other things.

The weather turned cold, so we didn't sit around on the porch like we did yesterday. After Catherine and I cleaned up the dishes, Mammaw let us have the table to do our project for social studies. Everybody in seventh grade was assigned a report about life in Kentucky. Some got environment for a topic, some got air quality, roads, natural resources, or about any other thing you could think of, but Catherine and I got festivals and celebrations, comparing the county where she lives with what we have around here.

I could see that her list was about five times longer than mine. I only had two festivals I could think of—the Daniel Boone Trailblazers Festival in the spring, and the Mountain Herb Festival in the fall. Catherine had the Bluegrass Classic Dog Show and the Champagne Run Horse Trials and the Clog Fest and I-don't-know-what-all. Her heart wasn't in it, though, and I noticed she kept reaching up to finger the gold locket around her neck.

It helped some that Ma sent Howard to bring me and Catherine down for a taffy pull. That's something Ma gets in her mind to do when somebody needs cheering up bad. Howard, of course, was all quiet and politeness, and Ezra and Danny'd already forgotten about Catherine's mama, just wanting to get their hands on a piece of that cooled syrup, laughing and giggling as they pulled it back and forth until it started to turn white and lose its shine.

I liked my family tonight. Even Daddy turned away from the TV, laughing at us. Sometimes I get to wondering, if we were to have just enough of what we need, not any more—if Daddy's truck could be repaired and Ma could get her teeth fixed and we could have us a new refrigerator and even a bathroom—would everybody be different? Or

would there be a whole new list of complaints?
Some of each, I'd guess. The rich folks on TV have
problems we never even heard of. Money can't buy
happiness, but it sure can make life a lot easier.

Ivy June Mosley

CHAPTER THIRTY-FOUR

April 6

I wish I were anywhere but here. How could the doctor not have known about Mom's heart problem? Or confused it with her pneumonia? Aren't we supposed to have the best in Lexington? Hasn't Dr. Wilson been with us forever?

All I get from Ivy June's family is old-fashioned reassurance. "There's always calm after a storm," "Trust the Lord," or "It's going to be okay." None of them know a single thing about what's going to happen to Mom. But then, I guess nobody back home does either.

How can people live this way—shut off up here in the hills without a phone? They'll spend their money on a satellite dish but go without a telephone. Why don't they form a protest and demand that the phone company put in a line? How can I stand not knowing what's going on all the time over in Cleveland? "That's just the way we live," Ivy June says. "The phone company'll get around to us by and by." They just accept things. Well, I don't!

And yet . . . at the taffy pull down at her mother's place, I was thinking how lucky it is that our family has health insurance. Her mom needs her teeth fixed and her dad has some kind of asthma. The only things they have to depend on are Jessie's paycheck and Mr. Mosley's dad, and he's sixty-four. If I were in that family, I think I'd be planning my escape as soon as possible. Go somewhere I could get through college and find a job. But there I am, judging again.

One thing, though. Even though I don't want to talk with them about my mom, because none of them say the right thing—and I don't even know what the right thing would be—I still want Ivy June near me.

I wonder how Claire and Peter are taking this, really. Wonder what Gramps has to say, and whether Rosemary says anything helpful at all. Tonight I'll hold Mom's locket and think good thoughts, and tomorrow Dad will call me at school. Meanwhile, at least I have Ivy June.

Catherine Combs

CHAPTER THIRTY-FIVE

On the bus Monday morning, Shirl was sitting with one of the girls this time, but in front of the row of boys, so that they were still reaching around the seat to tickle her or to snatch the baseball cap she liked to wear.

"Hi, Shirl," Ivy June said. "Why don't you sit with us at lunch?"

And Shirl looked her right in the eye this time and said, "Looks like you already got company."

"Got room for you!" Ivy June said, but Shirl grabbed at the boy who had taken her cap and never answered.

Ivy June wished right then that the bus wouldn't stop at the school. Wished it would just keep going on down the highway—four miles to the junction, past the turnoff to the mine where Papaw worked, on past the textile mill—and angle right down to Harlan. Not let anyone off till she and Shirl made up.

"She's mad at you because of me, isn't she?" Catherine asked Ivy June later.

"Oh, she'll get over it," Ivy June said, not really wanting to discuss it.

"Like you and me and Mackenzie," Catherine observed. "It's like Mom said once: 'Some friends are more fragile than others.' "

"She'll come around," Ivy June told her, and tried to think of other things.

The call came during English. Miss Dixon had been talking about Kentucky authors and the different types of writing they did, from mysteries to nonfiction, essays to novels. She wrote a few names on the board—*Carolyn Gordon, Elizabeth Hardwick, Robert Penn Warren, Sue Grafton, Barbara Kingsolver*—and assigned the class to come up with at least twenty more. Anyone who read a book by one of these authors by Friday would receive three extra points.

A speaker clicked on, and the school secretary said, "Miss Dixon, sorry for the interruption, but would you send Catherine Combs to the office, please?"

Everyone turned to look at Catherine, but she was out of her seat almost before her name was mentioned. Ivy June gave her an encouraging smile.

Five minutes went by. Then ten . . . twelve . . . Catherine still hadn't returned when the bell rang, and Ivy June headed toward the office. She met Catherine halfway down the hall. Catherine was smiling.

"Dad said she came through the operation okay," she said. "The doctor thinks it went well, and Dad said he'll call me again tomorrow."

"That's great!" Ivy June gave her a hug. "Oh, Cat, that's wonderful news, isn't it?"

"I hope so. I asked if this meant she was going to be all right, and Dad said that so far it looks good. Everyone's optimistic."

"Then so am I!" Ivy June told her. "Now don't you feel better?"

"Heaps. And I'm starved. I'm glad it's lunchtime," Catherine said.

"I wish you felt you could tell the other girls," Ivy June said.

"Maybe I will—now that I can talk about Mom without crying," Catherine said.

Ivy June hoped that this would help Shirl see Catherine in a different way. But Shirl didn't even walk by the table where Catherine and Ivy June were eating lunch, and when Catherine told the other girls about her mom's operation, Shirl wasn't there to hear.

"You must have been so worried!" said Angela.

"I'd be a basket case," said Mary Beth. "I'd want to be home in the worst way."

"I do," said Catherine. "Except that nobody's home. And Dad didn't want me sitting around in Cleveland."

Howard was waiting at the bus stop when they got off that afternoon. He was standing with his hands in his jeans pockets, his shoulders hunched against the wind. His eyes shifted from his feet to the girls and back again, and when he finally spoke, it seemed he was forcing himself to focus on Catherine.

"I . . . I hope your mom's okay," he said, his voice almost inaudible.

Catherine smiled. "She came through the operation all right. Dad called me this morning, and we talked for a long time."

Howard smiled shyly. "That's good," he said, and tagged along a couple of feet behind them as they started home.

They stopped off at Ma's to tell her, too. Ruth Mosley seemed genuinely happy for Catherine. "Nice to hear *some*thin's going right around here," she said. "That's good news for sure. I can guess you've been right worried. You girls want some sweet tea?"

Ivy June started to say that they wanted to get on up the hill to tell Mammaw but changed her mind: "Yeah, that would be nice, Ma."

"Got some sheet cake left that Jessie made," said her mother, and that brought Danny and Ezra running to the table.

Mammaw had prepared a good dinner that evening for whichever way the operation went, and gave Catherine a wide smile and a hug.

"Why, your ma may be better'n ever once she's recovered," she said. "Sometimes it takes a bad turn in life to bring the good. You take her back some of that sarsaparilla tea, Catherine, and it'll help keep her pressure down."

Grandmommy seemed to know that a celebration was in order, because she fingered the embroidered pocket of her cotton dress and said, "Got me my new dress on." When the girls told her how pretty she looked, she said it again.

The girls took over the table when it was cleared of dishes and attacked their homework assignments once again. They had used the computer in the school library for most of their social studies research, but would have to wait for the bookmobile to come around to get more books by Kentucky authors.

"I don't think I'll have time to read a book," Ivy June said. "I'm still trying to catch up on work I missed while I was away."

"We read a couple of Bobbie Ann Mason books last year," Catherine told her. "She wasn't on the list. And we read one of Barbara Kingsolver's books."

"Then you get three credit points not even trying!" exclaimed Ivy June.

"What's that you're workin' on?" Papaw asked,

coming out to the kitchen to get another dish of bread pudding. He peered down at the papers scattered about the table.

"Catherine and I have to write a paper on festivals in her county and mine," Ivy June told him. "What kind of festivals did you have growing up, Papaw?"

He chuckled and dipped his spoon in his bowl. "Well, we got together whenever we could, but nobody called it a festival. Maybe it'd be after a camp meeting in summertime, or neighbors coming together to shuck corn, or maybe we'd go to a hymn-sing. Any time the grown-ups got together was an excuse for the younguns to have a good time. And sometimes us kids got together for pure mischief."

"Like what? What did you do?" asked Catherine.

Papaw put the spoon to his mouth and savored the pudding on his tongue.

"Well, *I* never did this, now—lived too far from the rest—but on Halloween there were all kinds of ornery. In the middle of the night, they'd go get somebody's cow and lead it down to someone else's barn—git the other cow and bring it on back. Man would git up in the mornin' and find a strange cow waitin' to be milked. Swappin' cows. That was a favorite."

Ivy June and Catherine laughed loudly. "What else?" they asked.

"Well, the girls were always hangin' round to see what the fellers were up to, you know. Corn shuckings—why, the boy who found a red ear when he pulled off the husks, he got to kiss the girl of his choice. On the mouth, too. And that sure kept everyone busy. But if there was a new boy, we just weren't so nice. What was done to him was done to all of us, one time or another, but of course he didn't know that."

"What did you *do*?" Ivy June asked curiously.

Papaw gave her a guilty smile. "Us boys would invite him to a snipe hunt, and he's eager to fit in, see, so of course he'd go along."

"A *what* hunt?" asked Catherine.

Papaw just winked at her. "We'd wait till it was gettin' dark, and then we'd all go out in the woods, down in a gulley or somethin'. Give the new kid this big sack and tell him to stand real still and hold it open between his feet. That we were going to drive the snipe birds right down into the gully, and he was to collect 'em and bring 'em home."

"I never saw a snipe bird," said Ivy June.

Papaw chuckled. "Neither did we. That's the point. The boy, he's all eager to help on account of wanting to be one of the crowd. And then we'd go off, back to the house or the church or wherever the grown-ups were talking. We'd leave him standin' back there in the woods, holdin' the sack. And how we'd laugh when he'd finally come in, all sheepish-like, figuring out the trick."

"That was mean, Papaw," Ivy June said with a grin.

"Suppose it was. But any fella pass the snipe test, then he'd be in on the joke like the rest of us, and eager to try it on the next poor soul who come along."

"Did you ever have a bike? Anything like that?" Catherine asked.

"Hardly make it up these mountains if I'd had one," Papaw said. "Somebody made me a wagon once, I remember that. And we put a goat to it. Now, that was fun. For us, anyways. Not the goat."

Ivy June studied her list of festivals. "Did you ever take part in a greased pig contest or a terrapin race like they have over in Hayden? A coon-on-a-log competition, or a mudbog?"

"I expect there were things like that goin' on thereabouts, but we were pretty much left to our own devices." He grinned. "Anyone have a spare pig around, it would probably end up a ham on somebody's table, not a greased-up pig to play with."

That made Ivy June and Catherine both laugh.

"I don't expect you do much pig chasin' and snipe huntin' up your way," Papaw said to Catherine.

"Well, I never heard of any. But we've got the Bluegrass Classic Dog Show."

"Just a difference in animals, I guess," said Papaw.

◊◊◊

Ivy June was worried about Shirl. She'd always liked the boys, Shirley had, but this time the boy craziness seemed to be something more. Seemed to be aimed right smack at Ivy June, like it was both for real and for show. As though she was saying, *See what I got, Ivy June? I don't need you.*

Ivy June decided she should have given Shirl more warning of what it would be like when Catherine came to Thunder Creek. Should have explained that after Catherine went back to Lexington, Ivy June probably would never see her again. She was only treating Catherine Combs the same way she'd treat any kind of company, didn't matter where they were from. But Shirl could have figured that out for herself.

The problem was, if Ivy June and Shirl lived in Lexington, like Catherine did with her friends, Ivy June could have called Shirl on her cell phone and straightened things out. Sent her an e-mail message. Here in the hollow, there was no messaging back and forth. If the day ended and you weren't speaking, you couldn't set things right again till the next morning. And if you got on the bus and your best friend ignored you and sat back with the boys, then you somehow had to corner her during the day if you could and ask did she have something on her mind. And she'd say so, and still be mad for a while longer, till finally you both got sick and bored with it and made up.

When Ivy June dressed for school on Tuesday, she noticed Catherine pulling on a navy blue sweatshirt, so she purposely chose a green turtleneck for herself, making sure they didn't resemble each other.

Catherine aced the math test the teacher sprang on them that morning, but she fell behind a little in history, in their study of World War II. In geography, the girls were about even. Once again, she was called to the office for her dad's phone call, and once again, she came out smiling.

"Mom's awake and talking. She's on pain medication, but she told Dad she's glad it's over."

"And so are you," said Ivy June. "Do they know when she'll be going home?"

"They haven't said yet. Not for a while, I suppose."

At lunchtime, Shirl walked by their table but ate with someone else. At least she was getting closer, Ivy June thought wryly. She must have heard the news about Cat's mom. But the only classes that she and Catherine shared with Shirl were geography and science, and when Ivy June entered the science room after lunch, Shirl had her face in a book and didn't look up.

"Hope this isn't the day we're going to look at a frog's lungs," Ivy June said to no one in particular, something she'd been told was coming at some point in the semester.

"Well, I won't throw up if you don't," said Catherine.

Ivy June wasn't sure, but she thought she saw Shirl hide a smile.

A police car sped by the school, and Ivy June watched idly as another followed. Mrs. Toler up front raised her voice a little to get the students' attention, and Ivy June concentrated once more on the principles of heredity.

But then a car door slammed out in the parking lot, and Ivy June watched a woman jump from the car and run toward the office. Several other students noticed too. Then a rescue squad, its siren off, tore past the building.

Everyone watched the windows, even the teacher. At that moment, somebody's cell phone rang. Only a couple of kids had them, and cells weren't allowed in the classroom. But this time Mrs. Toler didn't object when George Wilson, a boy at the back, answered.

He listened, his face expressionless, lips parted, until finally he murmured, "Okay. . . ." Then he turned the phone off and stared for a moment at all the faces turned toward him. "It's the mine," he said. "Something's happened, but they won't tell us what."

Ivy June stood up, her notebook sliding to the floor.

"Class," Mrs. Toler said. "Let's just wait for an announcement from the office."

"My grandfather's down there," Ivy June said huskily, her dry lips sticking together as she tried to get the words out.

"So's my uncle," said George Wilson.

"I realize this is hard," the teacher said, "but we just don't know anything yet."

Other students rose and went to the windows. Ivy June and Catherine joined them. They stared in the direction of the mine, but there was no column of smoke rising over the hills, no cloud of dust in the air.

"I didn't hear an explosion," a girl told them.

But there were more sirens now, growing gradually louder. In the windows of the new wing, Ivy June could see other students staring at the sky.

The school intercom clicked on: "Students, there's

been an incident at the mine, and we're waiting for word from the sheriff's office," came the principal's voice. "Please remain in your classrooms, and as soon as we have any information, we'll announce it. Remain in your classrooms."

No one spoke. Some of the kids returned to their seats; others stayed at the windows. Waiting . . . waiting . . .

Mrs. Toler didn't seem to know what to do either. No topic in their textbook could match the importance of what might be happening just four miles down the road.

As the minutes ticked by, she asked finally, "How many of you have family at the mine?"

Two people, Ivy June and George Wilson, raised their hands. Luke Weller would have raised his hand if his dad were alive, Ivy June thought.

"How many *know* someone who works at the mine?" Mrs. Toler asked, and now almost every hand in the room went up. Shirl's hand went up too.

"Well, in a few minutes I'm sure we'll find out what's happened, and just how serious it is," the teacher said.

There didn't have to be an explosion for it to be serious, Ivy June knew. Didn't have to be a fire. There were small accidents just as deadly. But when not just an ambulance rode by, but police and rescue squads from places all around, you knew it was awful, and then there was another, then still another siren far off in the distance.

Someone in the office had turned the microphone on

before the principal was ready, because the class heard him say, "I can't announce that yet. . . ."

Another voice: "The mike's on, Mr. Gordon. . . ." A fumbling noise before the mike went dead.

Ivy June felt as though her hands and feet were turning to ice, and she shivered.

"This is so difficult," Mrs. Toler said sympathetically. No sound from the students. Then the microphone clicked on again.

"Students," came Mr. Gordon's voice, "there has been an accident at the mine, and at this point we are not sure just how serious it is or how many of the crew are involved. I know that this is an anxious time for those of you with relatives in the mine. I'm asking teachers to excuse those students from class. Please send them directly to the cafeteria and I'll meet them there. The rest of you should proceed with your lessons as planned."

George Wilson stood up, and so did Ivy June, her face pale. Catherine gathered up her and Ivy June's books, and Mrs. Toler nodded permission for Catherine to go along. Ivy June saw Luke Weller's eyes follow them toward the door.

"I'm praying for you," the teacher said as they left the room.

Ivy June knew her legs were moving, but they didn't seem to belong to her. With each step, her heart thumped painfully against the wall of her chest, as though any moment it would leap right out. She felt Catherine's arm around her waist.

Mr. Gordon was waiting just inside the door to the cafeteria, and he reached out to pat some of the students on the shoulders as they shuffled silently in. Sunlight streamed through the high windows, and Ivy June wondered how anything bad could happen on a day so cheerful-looking. For a moment she felt that Papaw just had to be all right. Then she saw the cafeteria women watching anxiously through the roll-up window back by the kitchen, and her heart pounded again.

"I wish I could tell you more," Mr. Gordon said, "but right now there hasn't been any statement from the mine. I've talked with someone at the sheriff's office, but they're not giving out details either. It is, they report, a serious situation, but right now we don't know who, if any—and I repeat—if *any* workers were hurt."

A panicky murmur went through the small crowd.

"But what *was* it?" someone called.

Mr. Gordon shook his head. "I don't know. We're calling each of your families to see if they want you to remain here, come home, or meet them at the Presbyterian church down there near the junction. That's where they're setting up a place for relatives to wait. We've got some volunteers who'll drive you there."

Students immediately began talking in low voices, turning to each other.

Mr. Gordon looked around. "Anyone here who doesn't have a phone at home?"

Ivy June and three others raised their hands.

"Okay, now. Sheriff's going to send somebody up to deliver the news, and I'm asking you to wait here till we know what your families want you to do."

Ma and Daddy and Mammaw and Grandmommy didn't know yet, Ivy June thought. Mammaw was probably out planting green beans, and then she'd see this stranger coming up the hill, or maybe Sam Feeley again, riding over on his horse.

Forty minutes there and forty back! she was thinking. She could not stay here not knowing. With Catherine following closely behind her, she zigzagged through the little crowd and over to where the principal was standing.

"Mr. Gordon, I want to go to that church. I know that's where my grandmother would tell me to go."

"You'll have to wait until we hear from her," the principal said, and turned to another girl who was pulling at his sleeve.

Ivy June wheeled around. She grabbed Catherine's arm, left the cafeteria, and headed for her locker.

CHAPTER THIRTY-SIX

"How far away is the mine?" Catherine asked cautiously. They had left their books in the locker.

"A ways," Ivy June said. "Four, five miles, maybe."

Catherine looked over at her. "It's like the teacher said, though. We really don't know anything yet." She waited. "I mean, your grandfather could be sitting outside the mine drinking a cup of coffee."

"You don't know that he is!" Ivy June shot back.

"But you don't know that he *isn't*," Catherine said. And then, "I'm sorry. I know how worried you are."

An ambulance sped by, but when the girls had walked another mile and it didn't return, Ivy June felt the panic again.

A car came up the road behind them and stopped. A policeman leaned toward the window. "You girls shouldn't be out this way," he called. "Going to be a lot of traffic coming by here."

Ivy June gave him a determined glance and kept walking.

The car moved forward and stopped again. "Hey! You hear what I'm tellin' you?"

Ivy June faced him. "My grandfather's down in that mine!" she said.

The officer's face softened. "Get in," he said. "I'll drive you to the church. That's where you'll get your information."

The small Presbyterian church was set back from the road, but already the parking area was filled with mud-splattered pickup trucks, old sedans, and here and there a newer model. A Red Cross van stood with its door open; a man lifted out a large coffee urn and carried it inside.

The policeman let the girls out, and Ivy June and Catherine walked across the lawn, the new grass peeking out between cars that were parked at an angle, leaving tire marks on the sod. Inside the door, a woman with a clipboard gently asked their names and the name of their relative working the mine.

"Spencer Mosley," Ivy June said. "My . . . my grandfather."

The woman touched her arm and nodded sympathetically. "As soon as they tell us anything, we'll let you know," she said.

Ivy June and Catherine sat down in the first row and

listened in on the conversations of people clustered about. The hard bench felt cold beneath them from the constant opening and closing of the door. A folding table off to one side held the coffee urn, which sat beside a large platter of store-bought cookies and a dish of potato salad. No one seemed to have answers to anything, only questions.

"How deep is the mine, Ivy June?" Catherine asked. "Do they know if the elevator's working? That ought to tell us something."

"It doesn't have an elevator. It's a drift mine—goes straight back into a hill from the side, not down."

Catherine's eyes brightened. "Well, that's good, isn't it? Couldn't the men walk out if they had to?"

"They could be two or three miles back," Ivy June said woodenly. "And there's all sorts of ways they could be . . . trapped."

The other miners' kids from school came in, driven there by volunteers.

"You find out anything?" George Wilson asked, sliding into the pew beside Ivy June.

"No," she told him, her voice shaky. "They're trying to get somebody from the mine to come talk to us."

Two men, a photographer and a reporter from the newspaper, entered the church, and people rushed over to ask what they knew. Nothing more, it turned out. The roadway to the mine had been closed off, and they were here to interview anxious relatives. Ivy June turned her face away.

Behind the sanctuary there were restrooms and a Bible study room, which appeared to be the command post for the volunteers and the newspeople. A couple of retired miners had taken it upon themselves to get reports from the mine officials and were scurrying around the room, talking on their cell phones. One of them, a white-haired man in a leather jacket, seemed to be the person relatives wanted most to talk to, but Ivy June could tell, when he shook his head, that he didn't know much more than anyone else.

"If there had been an explosion, wouldn't we have felt it?" someone said.

Ivy June knew what they were all thinking: fire, filling the passages and crossovers with fumes, sucking out the air and searing the lungs.

But another girl said, "My aunt lives a half mile from the mine, and she says there's no sign of smoke or anything, only rescue trucks."

"If it was a cave-in, I'll bet it was the tunnel left of the south entry. My uncle said last week that the roof needed shoring up, but nobody fixed it," said George Wilson.

Ivy June didn't want to hear that, and her heart raced. She'd heard Papaw say once that it wasn't the thought of death so much that made his blood turn cold—it was the fear of being trapped hundreds of feet inside a mountain with no way out.

". . . that slate come down on you, you don't even hear it," a man was saying.

Ivy June left the others and restlessly paced the room, stopping every so often to ask someone a question, but no one had an answer. The folding table at one side now supported a platter of sliced ham and a casserole of macaroni and cheese. The fragrance of fresh coffee filled her nostrils. But no one seemed to be eating except the photographer, who made a sandwich out of ham and a roll, then hurried on out to his car.

"Ivy June!"

Ivy June wheeled about, and there was Mammaw, a frenzied look on her face. Ivy June was shocked when her grandmother grabbed her by the shoulders and shook her.

"W-what?" Ivy June stammered.

"Where you been? I've not enough on my mind to worry about?" Mammaw declared, and suddenly she pulled Ivy June toward her and hugged her, crying.

Daddy came in the door, his face drawn. "Mrs. Murphy came up to get us, Ivy June, and said we were to stop by the school and pick you up. Mr. Gordon, he didn't know where you was, or Catherine, neither. Said you were told to wait in the cafeteria till we got there."

"I . . . I couldn't," Ivy June said. "I just c-couldn't."

"They saying anything yet?"

"No. Where was Papaw working, Mammaw? What tunnel was he in?"

Mammaw shook her head. "I don't know, I don't know. Week before, he was working the north main, but he just didn't say. . . ."

"Sit down, Ma," Daddy told her. "Don't upset yourself any more. We forgot your nerve medicine, remember."

"Lord, and I-don't-know-what-all," Mammaw said,

lowering herself onto a pew, then grabbing at Catherine's hand as Cat saw the family and came over. "Ruth's there at the house with the boys looking after Grandmommy, and Jessie, I 'spect, will be here shortly, she hears the news." Mammaw dug in her sweater pocket for a handkerchief and wiped her eyes.

Catherine sat down in the pew in front, turned so she could talk with them. She looked helpless and out of place, but Ivy June could feel nothing for Catherine just then, could feel only her own terror and helplessness.

Off in the distance, they could hear a siren coming—from the direction not of the town but of the mine. Everyone pivoted toward the door as the ambulance raced past, the flash of its red light momentarily spotting the walls of the church. That meant that *some*one was alive.

The white-haired man in the leather jacket, holding a cell phone to his ear, limped to the front of the sanctuary. Ivy June could tell he'd been a miner—the nicks on his cheekbones and the bridge of his nose where rock had fallen. Miners' tattoos, folks called them. People immediately surged toward him, but he pocketed the cell phone and held up one hand. An immediate hush fell over the room.

"I'm going to give it to you straight, folks, and this is all I know," he said. "Charlie Sizemore's at the mine now, and we're going to keep trading places till—"

"Just get on with it, Brady!" a man called out.

The white-haired man nodded, and his face looked

243

pained. "There's been a flood at the mine. They drilled into water."

Gasps and cries traveled around the room.

"Oh, my Lord Jesus . . . ," murmured Mammaw.

The man named Brady continued: "There were twenty-nine men on the morning shift, and seven of them working the north passages. Three men were in the number one room, four working the number two. One of the men, Les Crowley, was washed out into the main entry and was grabbed by another miner near the mouth. They escaped by riding the conveyor belt the rest of the way out."

"Who pulled Les out?" a woman called.

"I don't know, but Crowley's on his way to the hospital and he's conscious, so maybe he'll be able to tell us what happened. We're guessing somebody cut into trapped water. They've got one pump going and more equipment on the way."

"Just one pump?" someone shouted.

The room was filled with more questions, exclamations, but all Ivy June heard right then was Mammaw's breathless "Spencer can't swim."

A man standing next to Brady held up his hand for attention: "Remember, y'all, Brady used to work at the mine, so don't hold him accountable. If it wasn't for him, we wouldn't have no news a'tall."

The crowd quieted some then.

"What about the men working the south passages?" somebody asked.

"They've got nineteen men up the main straight trapped on high ground, and they've been told to stay put till the pumps bring the water down," Brady said. Then, "Hold on a minute." His cell phone was ringing and he held it to his ear. Then he turned once more toward the crowd and said, "The second man on the conveyor belt was Smit Wilson, and he's okay."

"Hey, George!" some of the kids cried, and Ivy June saw the relief on the boy's face.

"Give us the names of the men they know are alive," a woman pleaded.

"We're trying to get that now. Charlie's down at the mine checking. As soon as he calls, I'll tape the names on the door back there," Brady said, motioning to the Bible study room.

Ivy June clutched her daddy's arm. "Where could all that water come from, Daddy? Underground river or something?"

"Probably an abandoned mine next to this one," he said. "Sometimes they fill up."

"And nobody knew it was there?" Ivy June said, angry tears filling her eyes.

Someone else asked the question: "How come they didn't know water was there? How come they was drilling where it wasn't safe?"

"We'd all like to know that," Brady said. "Could be they had a faulty map, or management didn't do an accurate survey—I'm not the one to ask."

"Is there a rescue team there now?" Daddy called out.

"They've called for one, but I don't know who they've got," said Brady. "They don't get here soon, I swear I'll go in there myself."

Ivy June tried to imagine her grandfather crawling to escape the rush of water, when it even took him a while now to get up out of a chair.

Most of the time, he'd told her once, he was squatting down or bending over in tunnels not more than four feet high. Or he was crawling on his hands and knees. A sixty-four-year-old man had no business at all doing something like that. If it was the big coal company he'd worked for as a young man, he'd said, they wouldn't have taken him on at this age. But when they had mined what they wanted and closed operations, they'd sold to a small company that went in to get what was left. The small company wanted experienced men, and if you had a pulse, Papaw once said, they'd take you, long as you didn't complain.

Why *hadn't* he complained? Ivy June wondered. Why hadn't he done something else? Each time he went into the mountain, he was taking a chance.

She cried.

Darkness fell, and a cold rain drummed on the church roof. More casseroles arrived, along with cakes and freshly baked pies. The sanctuary smelled of fried chicken, sausage and sauerkraut, wet concrete, and mud from the boots of men who tramped back and forth from their

246

fruitless trips to the mine. Many relatives sat in their cars outside the church, too numb to come inside, listening for news on their car radios.

Catherine tried to help out by dialing the mine office herself on her cell phone. If they answered, she was ready to hand the phone to Ivy June's dad. But always the line was busy, as Brady had warned them all that it would be.

Feeling she could no longer stand the suspense, Ivy June got up to use the restroom, then impulsively walked out the side door and set out blindly along the road toward the mine, pulling her jacket up over her head. But when she reached the roadblock, a policeman stopped her.

"Where you headed, miss?" he asked, aiming his flashlight in her direction.

"My grandfather's down there," she said, weeping.

"I'm sorry, but only emergency crews can go by right now," he told her. "We've got some bulldozers coming to clear a path for a drill rig."

"You don't know what it's like!" Ivy June said angrily. "Just waiting and waiting and not knowing anything . . ."

"Well," he said, "I do know what it's like. My son's down there."

Ivy June stopped, chastened, and then, unable even to say she was sorry, she turned away, her tears mixing with rain. Her father was coming toward her.

"Come inside, girl," he said, leading her back toward the church.

"Daddy," she cried in a small voice, "if anything happens to Papaw, what are we going to do?" And as soon as she said it, she regretted the question, for, looking up, she saw that her daddy's face was as sorrowful as she'd ever seen it. He didn't answer, only squeezed her hand.

How could this be happening the day after Catherine's mom had her operation? What were the chances that these two girls, the only ones in the exchange program—the first Thunder Creek had ever had—would have something bad happen to their families almost on the same day? Trouble wasn't supposed to come in fours, with the fourth being worst of all! It didn't make sense, it wasn't fair, it wasn't even likely, and yet—it was real.

Catherine was standing on the church steps, motioning toward them. "Come inside!" she called. "They're going to read names."

Daddy sat down in the pew beside Mammaw, Ivy June next to him and Catherine on the end.

Brady stood before them, holding a sheet of paper. His face was grave, and the room was still as a mountain.

"I just got back from the mine," he said, "and here's what we know: we have three miners aboveground, including Smit Wilson and Les Crowley; Tom Reeves is the third. Got nineteen men trapped but alive and accounted for—they got through once on the voice-activated phone—five men missing, and two men dead. The families of the two have been notified, and I'm sorry to report the names of Easter Preston and Mose Hardy."

"Not Mose!" Mammaw gasped.

Some people began to cry. It was a name—both names—that Ivy June had heard mentioned now and then. She could not even blink. She waited.

"Here are the five who are missing," Brady continued. "And remember, folks, there are lots of places these men might be." He looked down at the list again. "Eldon Potter, Ted Hatfield, Eli Dodd, Spencer Mosley, and Bill McClung."

"Oh, Ivy June!" said Catherine. But Ivy June had her face buried in her daddy's sleeve, and he embraced his mother.

◊◊◊

The Red Cross set up some cots at the back of the sanctuary, and a few more down by the altar. They also handed out blankets and aspirin.

Lying on a wooden pew, Ivy June made a pillow of her blanket, then shared head space on it with Catherine, each girl pointed in the opposite direction.

Ivy June didn't think she could sleep. Wondered if she would ever sleep again, but woke only once in the night when she felt someone cover her up. She opened her eyes in the morning to the sound of rain still falling and saw that her daddy had placed his jacket around her shoulders. Mammaw slumped in one corner, her head tilted back, a pillow under her neck, snoring softly.

When Ivy June went to the restroom at the back of the church, she found a bottle of mouthwash and paper cups, courtesy again of the Red Cross. She and Catherine drank orange juice at the long table, now bearing doughnuts and sticky buns. Mammaw woke, and while Catherine was putting together a breakfast for her, Ivy June went outside to look for her father. He was there on the front steps, smoking, talking to the other men.

"Any news?" she asked.

Daddy shook his head.

"Least they're lettin' some of us past the barricade now," one man said. "They got four turbine pumps going, and a borehole going to the nineteen men trapped in the south tunnel, 'cause that voice-activated phone they got down there keeps goin' out."

"And . . . the men in the north tunnel?" Ivy June asked.

Daddy shook his head. "There've been no other bodies washed out, Ivy June. That's all we know."

The morning, and all the miners' relatives with it, seemed to move in slow motion. Each time Catherine called the mine office, the line was busy. Finally, her cell phone battery gave out.

Ivy June's legs were stiff and achy, and she felt groggy. She ate, not because she was hungry, but to stop the pains in her stomach. When Catherine offered to brush her hair, Ivy June sat still and closed her eyes to the brush-strokes, like a small child obeying orders.

Then, when the rain let up, Ivy June took a slow walk around the cars in the parking lot. She was heading back inside when someone grabbed her around the waist. She turned and found herself in Shirley's arms. Her friend hugged her hard.

"Ivy June, I'm so sorry." Shirl sniffled. "Lord, I'm sorry."

"I know," Ivy June gulped, hugging her back. When they finally let go, Ivy June asked, "Is it still Wednesday?"

"Wednesday, twelve o'clock," Shirl answered.

"What are you doing out of school?"

This time a smile played around Shirl's lips. "Always wanted to skip, and figured this was as good an excuse as any." She grew serious again. "Anyway, I wanted to find you."

"I see somebody over there waving at you," Ivy June told her, noticing a beat-up Chevy on the road in front of the church; then she recognized Fred Mason in the front seat beside an older boy who was driving.

"Yeah, me and Fred are going to the Big Happy for lunch with his cousin. Lots of kids skipping. Whole town's torn up over this. You want to go with us? Get your mind off things for a little while?"

Ivy June shook her head. "No, you go. I know you'll come back, once we've heard."

Shirl nodded and hugged her again, then walked off toward the Chevy.

Ivy June made one more lap around the parking lot, watching the car drive off. She wanted in the worst way to be one of the laughing girls at the Big Happy Sub Shop, watching some customer try to eat the four-foot sub all by himself and win a supersize T-shirt. Wanted to be in a car with somebody—boys, even—laughing, going places. But wishes wouldn't help.

))((

Mrs. Hedges, a neighbor from Vulture's Pass, leaned over Mammaw there in the pew. "Emma, I'm going up to the house to make some chicken and rice to bring back tonight. I could stop off at your house and fetch whatever you like, you needing something."

Mammaw's eyes were tired and so was her voice. "Thank you so much, Naomi. Russell's not got himself another truck yet, so we haven't a way back and forth. Jessie was here last night on her way home from work but hadn't a thing with her we could use. I need my medicine— Ruth'll give it to you—and something warm for my feet. My knee-high boots, maybe. And my old green jacket behind the door."

Catherine heard and walked over. "I could go up with her, Mammaw, and help. I need some of my stuff, and the battery charger for my cell phone so I can call Dad." She turned to Ivy June, who was resting her head on one arm. "Anything you want me to bring back?"

"We'll be home tomorrow," Ivy June said, her eyelids heavy, her voice flat. "The water's going down all the time, and we'll be home."

Catherine looked at Mammaw. "I'll see what I can find," she said.

))((

News reports came from the mine all afternoon and evening. First the man named Charlie posted them on the door of the Bible study room. Then Brady. Water had filled the whole mile and a half of twisting passages and chambers of the mine, like a huge underground lake. The rescue workers were now pumping water from several different places, and the water had begun to recede. Through a test hole, the men trapped in the main straight reported they were all right. Morale was high, and rescuers had even heard them singing. But when they drilled test holes to the north passages, all they got was water.

Ivy June curled up at the end of the pew, one blanket under her head, another tucked around her body. She was shivering, not because she was cold, but because she was thinking of cold. Of water and air of fifty-nine degrees. Of mud and rock, and how much food was in Papaw's lunch bucket. How long the battery-operated lamp on his helmet would work.

And then Catherine was kneeling beside her.

"I'm back," she said. "I got some clean clothes for you, your toothbrush and paste. Brought some pillows, too. And this." She took Ivy June's hand and put something in it. It was small and hard, rough on one side, smooth on the other. Ivy June closed her fingers around it and drew her hand back under the blanket.

CHAPTER THIRTY-SEVEN

April 11

 It's been five days since I wrote in my journal,
and for Ivy June, it must seem like a year. She's
been in that church since Tuesday, and it's Friday
now. Miss Dixon drove us to her house once so we
could shower, but we're back now, and Ivy June
says she's staying till her Papaw walks out of that
mine. I picked up my journal when I was back
at the house, and I'm trying to write down
everything I see and hear. With Mr. Mosley in the
mine and Mom in the hospital, things don't seem
real.

 It's so strange that, here in the town of
Thunder Creek, I can talk to my mom in

Cleveland by cell phone, but Ivy June can't even call home. Dad thinks Mom won't be out of the hospital till next Thursday. She's doing fine, but her surgery was complicated, he said, and the doctors want her to stay there in Cleveland for about ten days. I've got so many questions, but Dad's answered what he can. So I concentrate on Ivy June's grandfather.

Yesterday I went to the mine with her and her daddy and Mammaw just so they could see for themselves that the pumps were working as fast as they could go. We listened to the mine officials explain how they're doing all they can. There are so many people gathered there now that they're only letting families of the miners in. Ivy June said I was her sister so I could go too.

About all I saw was this huge gaping hole that was the entrance, with a conveyor belt where the coal comes out. Pumps were going and water was gushing, and men in helmets were getting instructions on walkie-talkies.

Mostly, there were just two ambulances standing by, and people trying to look busy, when they really can't do anything till the water level goes down. There are long stretches of water that rescue workers can't get through, someone explained. They've waterproofed packages of food and sent them through the tunnel on a conveyor belt to the men in the south tunnel.

It really doesn't sound good for Ivy June's grandfather. They say the only places the men in the north tunnel could have escaped to are the number three and four rooms, but they drilled test holes and pounded on the steel drill pipe for a long time and no one answered. They even put a siren over one hole and played that for twenty minutes, but all they got back was silence. Ivy June cried on Mammaw's shoulder but she still won't give up, and neither will her daddy or grandmother.

What everyone talks about here is hope, like it's a safety line you can hang on to. Ministers come by the church and talk to the families, reading Scripture and praying with them. They tell them to have faith that the miners are alive in body or alive in Christ, and either is cause for celebration. I don't know. . . .

If the water level goes down enough by tonight, rescue workers will go in just to see if the tunnel's clear and then will bring out the men in the south tunnel. Already women are gathering at the mouth of the mine, reporters tell us, and one kid is carrying a bunch of balloons for his dad. Some of the women have fresh clothes for the men. It's the relatives back here at the church who won't see their men tonight. I heard a rumor that the officials are going to send in body bags when a rescue team goes in the north tunnel, but I'm not telling Ivy June. It will still be another day or two, they said, before the water will be low enough for anyone to go in there at all.

I'm sitting here in the pew behind Ivy June right now, and I think she's asleep. Hope so, anyway. But it's awful to be asleep and dream of somebody and then wake up and remember what's happened. Ivy June's grandma is asleep on a cot next to the wall, and her dad went home for a few hours to see how Mrs. Mosley's getting along with Grandmommy and the boys. Jessie's got no choice but to keep working.

I'll be home when Mom comes back from the hospital, but until then, I'll stay with Ivy June as long as I can. Mom says I should. But the things I said last Saturday to Ivy June up on the ridge! How much was true, and how much was I just upset about Mom? When the exchange program is over, I'm supposed to go back to Lexington and share as much of my journal as I want with my class. We're supposed to talk about real differences and perceived differences, and . . . I just don't know. Sadness feels the same, whether it's in Lexington or here in Thunder Creek.

One of the differences between my family and Ivy June's is that in hers, every last child is expected to help in some way. Ivy June's always got a bunch of jobs waiting for her as soon as she gets home from school. And if we stop off at her ma's first, Howard and Ezra and even little Danny have chores to get done before dinner.

Peter and Claire and I . . . we're loved, I know . . . but I don't have the feeling we're really needed. Dad and Mom need us to make up the family, I suppose, but it's not like if we were to disappear tomorrow, there would be work that didn't get done.

Here in Thunder Creek, it's like a big family. Like everyone is related, even the people in towns a hundred miles away. Women who have gone home to make welcome signs for the men in the south tunnels come back to church with hot suppers for the relatives of the men in the north tunnels. Blankets, too. I've counted more patchwork quilts than Red Cross blankets.

I'd like to think that if there were some big catastrophe back in Lexington, our neighbors would do the same. Strangers, even. That they'd strip the blankets off their beds and bring us food off their tables, sit and hold our hands and hug us whether they knew us or not. The same

258

mountains that separate these people from the rest
of the world seem to keep them close to each
other, and for that, I wonder if Ivy June knows
just how lucky she is.

Catherine Combs

CHAPTER THIRTY-EIGHT

Ivy June did not go to the mine when the men from the south passages were rescued. The photographers and reporters were there, of course. Brady, the old retired miner, went as well, but he came back afterward to sit quietly with the relatives of the missing miners.

"What do the men from the south passages know about the five who are missing?" Daddy asked him.

Brady shook his head. "Nothing. The way they tell it, water came rushing down the tunnel, sweeping away everything in its path. Heard men yell, "Water! It's water!" and it filled their room ankle deep before it washed on down the passage. Thought they could wade out, but there was a low place at least a hundred feet long and filled to the top with water. So they stayed put till the rescuers got to 'em; but that tells us just how deep the water is."

The little group of relatives was silent. The jubilation that they knew was taking place back at the mine made their grief that much sharper. Jessie had come that morning and stayed with Mammaw throughout the day, and she gently massaged the elderly woman's neck and shoulders as they listened to Brady. The grayness in the church was getting darker. The Red Cross was still there. Food kept arriving; the table was full. But the faces of the waiting relatives were heavy with fatigue, and their voices were almost inaudible.

"They trying to tell us there's no hope?" one woman asked, but the others glanced at her sharply.

Brady sighed. "It doesn't look good."

"When . . . will we know?" asked Mammaw.

"Well, they're pumping out three thousand gallons a minute, but it'll be another day or two before they can get the rescue team in that part. Even got some skin divers standing by, but some of those tunnels aren't more'n thirty inches high, water up to the roof. Divers can't get their equipment through there."

"But the rescue team *will* go in, won't it?" Jessie said. "They won't just . . . ?"

"They'll go in regardless, if I have to go in there myself," Brady promised. "No miner leaves another in the hole if there's any way in the world to get him out."

᪡

Ivy June lay down on a cot early that evening and slept as long as she could the next morning, even though the cot

261

was not much more comfortable than the wood pew where she'd been camped out.

"What day is it?" she asked her grandmother when she opened her eyes at last.

"Sunday," Mammaw said. "Preacher here says to just stay put—the service this mornin' will be for ministerin' to others."

The little congregation took Pastor Gordon's message to heart, for all morning people arrived with bowls and baskets of food. They offered to take relatives to their nearby homes to shower and freshen up. Take a nap in a real bed if they liked. Brought soap and toothpaste and still more blankets for those who refused to leave. Ivy June and Catherine went once to Shirl's aunt's house to bathe, then came back to the church, still sleepy-eyed, but clean. They listened while Shirl chatted softly with other friends from school who came to sit with the family, but it was hard for Ivy June to concentrate.

Jimmy Harris came too. He sat awkwardly on the low step by the altar, arms resting on his knees.

"Anyway," he said finally, his glance taking in the platter of large brownies someone had just delivered to the food table, "I sure hope they find the men soon."

Ivy June nodded, but she hated this. She did not *want* all this attention. Did not want to be the girl who was pitied, the one with her stomach aching because she could not eat, her throat rejecting any thought of food. She did not want to have to stay here after her friends had offered their sympathy, and could not stand the haunting thought that she might have to go through all this again at a funeral.

When Jimmy Harris left, he veered slightly toward the food table, then must have thought better of it, for he went on outside, where his buddies were waiting.

Four different ministers stopped by the church that day to visit with families. But every now and then, Ivy June and Catherine went outside to do their silent walk around the perimeter of the church grounds, down the road to the mine and back.

"Is it still Sunday?" Ivy June asked once, hardly feeling her feet take the steps. She concentrated on Catherine suddenly: "Cat, you were supposed to go home yesterday!"

"I wanted to be here," Catherine told her. "I'd like to stay until they find the men, but I've got to go back by Wednesday. Mom's coming home the next day."

"Of course! You've got to be there then!" Ivy June agreed. "Oh, Cat, how do you stand this—all this sadness?"

Catherine just slipped an arm around her. "How do *you?*" she asked.

※

Monday. School buses rattled by on the road as though life were going on same as always. The white petals of the bloodroot plant spotted the hillsides, their bright yellow centers like little sunbursts. The gardenia-like anemones had come to life along with the new green of spring.

Wildflowers popped up here and there, even between rusty pickups deserted by the side of the road and old tires resting in ditches.

Mammaw slept long and deeply, rolled up in a blanket on a pew, and Daddy drove Papaw's car home from the mine to check on Ma and Grandmommy and the boys. When he came back, he brought Howard, who had ditched school.

"I shoulda been here all along!" Howard protested. "I'm old enough."

"It's that you're as old as you are, we wanted you home in case your ma needed you," Daddy told him. "If you can keep your mammaw company, you can stay till Jessie comes after work, but then you got to go home again with her."

Howard obediently settled next to Mammaw and asked if she wanted something to drink. Then he noticed the table with all the food. "That for us?" he asked.

Mammaw gave him a small smile as she took the comb out of her hair and tried to rebraid the bun. "Help yourself, Howard, but don't be touching anything you're not planning to eat," she said.

Ivy June was half asleep and Catherine was reading a book that Miss Dixon had left for them when suddenly the man named Charlie came dashing out of the Bible study room in back.

"Someone's been heard!" he called out, astonished.

Heads turned.

"What?" said Daddy, getting to his feet.

"Brady just called. The rescue team is down there and they think they heard somebody!"

Stunned, people turned toward each other.

Another old miner shook his head. "Could be anything," he said. "Could be water sloshin' against an oil drum or somethin'."

"No! Voices. A voice, anyway," Charlie said.

"Oh, Lord, make it true!" a woman cried.

"All I'm saying is, don't get your hopes up, but we think someone else is alive," Charlie told them.

"Remember Sago," the old miner murmured, referring to an accident at a mine in West Virginia. "Told 'em all thirteen men was alive, and folks started dancin' before the news came that they was all dead but one. . . ."

But he was shouted down now by the others.

"I'm going to the mine and see for myself," said someone, and suddenly people were reaching for their shoes and their jackets, setting down their cups of coffee and fumbling for car keys.

The Red Cross volunteers buzzed among themselves, chattering about what to wrap up and take to the mine, in case there should be another long wait there. A car engine started up out front, then another.

Mammaw hastily jabbed her comb back in her hair, one piece of braid dangling. Daddy thrust his long arms into the sleeves of his old sweater, then into his jacket. Ivy June was already on her feet, Catherine dropped her book, and Howard was at the church door calling, "Hurry! Come on, Daddy! I want to go!"

Now vehicles were streaming toward the mine entrance—Ford pickups, Dodge minivans, Toyota Camrys—
and after parking, relatives hurried toward the low
aluminum-sided building with the weathered OFFICE sign
on the door.

Fifteen minutes before, rescue workers had mostly
stood about waiting for the water to go down. Now men
were running, yelling to each other, their voices tight
with excitement. Miners were heading for the conveyor
belt opening, slipping and sliding in the mud.

Brady came running over. "There's somebody down
there," he yelled, "and men are going through. Water's
about eighteen inches, and they think they can make it, if
they don't hit a swag. Can't tell yet who's back there, but
Pete Osler says he heard a voice. He yelled and there's an
answer from somebody."

"Who? Who?" people screamed.

"Too far away to make out any words, but Pete says it's
no fool echo."

More news was coming through, being relayed to the
rescue worker at another voice-activated phone deep in
the tunnel. That phone connected to the man at the
mine entrance, who passed each message on to the officials standing nearby. And because the determined crowd
was converging on them, the officials passed on to Brady
and the other miners as much information as they could.
Reporters pressed forward, and another ambulance entered the mine gate, light blinking, siren off.

"If one's alive, it might mean there are more!" Ivy

June told Catherine, tightly squeezing her fingers around the little rock in her jacket pocket. "It could happen!"

Now there were shouts from the men at the mine entrance. The crowd murmured expectantly, waiting for the man by the conveyor belt to repeat what was coming to him by phone. Whatever the official was hearing, he wasn't telling, but Brady wound his way over and soon came back with the latest:

"It's slow going. There's a real low place, and looks like the water's blocked the tunnel, but I don't think they'd have heard voices if it was roofed."

Ivy June shivered. Hope rose and fell in her chest like water surging, then receding again.

One of the men at the tunnel entrance gave a little laugh and looked about: "Pete says a sandwich bag just floated by." And when people stared at him, he added, "Not that it means anything, but it's empty."

The line was repeated again and again, the news traveling from one little cluster of relatives to another. *A sandwich bag . . . an empty sandwich bag . . .*

Now Ivy June could not see the man at the entrance any longer, for more officials had come out of the office and were asking the reporters and photographers to move back. Fifteen more minutes . . . twenty . . . Mammaw leaned against Daddy, and he asked if she wanted to go back to the car and sit down.

"I'm stayin' right here till my Spencer walks up to me," she said.

And then, despite the caution of the officials, the

267

rescue workers there by the conveyor belt gave a shout, a cheer.

"We got 'em!" came the cry.

"Who? Who?" people yelled.

"*All* of 'em!" was the reply.

The crowd screamed. People fell into each other's arms the way they did on New Year's Eve on TV, Ivy June thought. She was engulfed in her daddy's arms, then Mammaw's, then Catherine's, and—she discovered in astonishment—she was even hugging Howard.

〰️

Ivy June remembered the day Danny was born because he'd been born at home, and she had helped. She remembered a blizzard that had started up one afternoon when she and Howard were halfway home from school, and how they'd fallen down twice in the snow. She remembered another time when the Middle Fork of the Kentucky River had flooded and they hadn't gone to school for a week, and she remembered the Christmas she'd gotten the red jacket she'd seen at Walmart.

But no day, no moment, was as fine as the sight of Papaw, his clothes covered with mud and slime, his face so dirty she could only make out the whites of his eyes, when he came out of that dark black hole, one hand holding on to the conveyor belt, the other holding on to his rescuer.

The crowd, swollen now to several hundred, cheered

for every man in turn. Reporters crowded the entrance; cameras flashed. The Red Cross was there with towels and hot coffee and sandwiches, and a doctor gave each man a quick check to see who needed a hospital. Hospital or home, each miner, dehydrated, his legs shaky and un-used to standing, got a shower if he wanted, and then a ride all the way home in an ambulance. Mammaw joined Papaw inside.

Mammaw was too exhausted to cook, but she didn't need to. Ivy June's ma had a dinner all ready for them. People had been driving all the way back into the hollow to give her the news and to bring a dish of their own for Papaw's supper.

Papaw sat in his old recliner chair by the coal stove, his stubbled face lined with weariness, eyes half-closed, but smiling nonetheless. But it wasn't until he'd slept for two hours and the family had gathered for dinner that he found the energy to tell them what had happened that day in the mine.

"Lord, look at all this food!" Mammaw exclaimed as the family took their heaping plates into the parlor and perched on every available table and chair. "Pie, cake, cookies—I-don't-know-what-all."

And Papaw said, "Just bein' home is all the sweets I need for the rest of my life." And Mammaw kissed him on the mouth, making even Ezra stare.

The question they all wanted answered was how had the men survived? The number two room, where they had been found, was even lower down than the number one room, where the auger had cut through to water. And the number one room, the rescue team had discovered when they drilled, was filled to the roof with water.

"Must have been a great big air bubble that saved us," Papaw said. "That's all we can figure. Two of the men, the one workin' the machine and the man who was with 'im, were washed away. But the rest of us heard a yell, and we turned around to see a third man tumblin' head over heels into our room.

"I grabbed his arm with one hand, my lunch bucket with the other, and all of us scrambled to the highest part, roof not thirty inches above our heads. We're squattin' up there, looking down at that water rising below us, and you don't know fear till you've lived with that, I tell you."

Ivy June tried to imagine her grandfather, all six feet two of him, crouched on that ledge for six days.

"Our best guess is that water rushed in so fast it pushed all the air into the top of the number two room, but we didn't know how much water there would be, how far up it would come before it stopped. We turned off our helmet lamps to save the batteries, but every so often one of us would turn his on just to see how high it had come."

"How deep did it get?" asked Daddy.

"Twenty inches, maybe. But we knew that was deep enough to swamp the low places in the tunnel and there was nothing to do but wait for the rescue and pray they knew where we were. At least we knew we had a chance. Then we took stock of how many lunch buckets were saved, and between the five of us there were six sandwiches, a quart of milk, three quarts of water, a piece of cheese, a handful of cookies, and two candy bars."

"Oh, Spencer, if I'd known, I'd have packed you a feast that morning!" exclaimed Mammaw, and somehow that made people laugh. All but Grandmommy, Ivy June noticed. Jessie had parked her great-grandmother's wheelchair right up next to Papaw's recliner, and every so often Grandmommy reached out her thin fingers and grasped at Papaw's arm, and he stroked her hand in reassurance.

"We knew that if the water went down some, we could probably crawl out," Papaw said. "What worried us more than whether our food would hold out was whether we'd have enough air for as long as we were there. And cold . . . oh, but we were cold. Slept belly to belly and back to back, and didn't seem like our clothes would ever get dry."

"Did you ever check to see if you could get out yet?" Howard asked.

"Couple times, but all it did was get our clothes wet all over again. We'd send somebody out, and he'd get to where the whole tunnel was underwater and have to come back. When we heard that rescue team, old Pete's voice hollerin' for us, we were singin' and shoutin' and arm-dancin' with each other—sweetest sound in the world to hear a yell when you think they've given up on you."

"We would never give up on you!" Ivy June declared.

"They said they drilled holes, Papaw, and hammered and pounded, but nobody pounded back."

"Well, they drilled and hammered in the wrong place, then, because we never heard 'em," Papaw said. "If they *had* drilled into the number two room, the air would have gotten out, and like as not, the water would have risen and drowned us before we could even let them know we were there. But we were ready to crawl out, we got the chance." He winked at Catherine. "When you go back to Lexington, you tell 'em we're a tough lot down here. You don't work inside the earth without a part of you turnin' to rock."

"But not your heart, Spencer," said Mammaw.

"No," he said. "Not my heart." He rubbed the back of his neck and moved his head from side to side. "Don't know that I'll ever get this crick out of my neck. One part of that roof was so low up over the ledge we had to lie down under it. Had to turn on our sides to drink water."

"I bet I could do it!" Howard said. "If I had to live for a week not able to sit up, I bet I could do it if I had enough food."

"Don't you be talkin' like that!" Ruth Mosley snapped. "You get into enough mischief here without doing your nonsense down in a mine."

"Then I'll get me a truck and help Daddy pick up scrap metal," Howard said, wanting to see some kind of future for himself. "Get a big enough truck, we could pick up twice as much."

"Howard, you mind your studies and stay in school, you won't have to do either one," said Mammaw. "Now where's that celebration cake Mrs. Hedges brought down?"

She got up, went to the kitchen, and returned with a coconut cake. "Guess this will serve as the welcome home for your granddaddy and our goodbye to Catherine," she said, " 'cause I 'spect she'll be wanting to go home soon as she can, see her ma." Everyone turned to look at Catherine, as though she had suddenly reappeared after a long absence.

"I'll go back tomorrow if I can," Catherine said. "Mom's coming home Thursday, and there's a lot to do."

"Miss Dixon said she'll drive you the very minute you want to go," Mammaw told her. "Now, who gets the first slice of this coconut cake?"

Papaw closed his eyes, still smiling. "Just slice it, Emma, and let everyone have a piece. This old stomach of mine has to get used to having food in it again."

ꕥ

The girls got up half an hour early the next morning because Ivy June knew that Catherine would never get out of the house with just a short goodbye.

Mammaw insisted on packing a little bag with dried-apple pies in case Catherine got hungry on her way to Lexington that afternoon, and Grandmommy had to recount all that had happened in the past two weeks, as though Catherine hadn't been here to see for herself.

Grandmommy's tale kept coming back to her son Spencer, however, and his rescue at the mine, which she attributed to the good life Papaw had led: "If you do what's right," she said, "then at the end of your life . . . you can lie down . . . and be peaceful with yourself."

"That's right, Iree, but Spencer's not about to lie down. He's got that garden to plant," Mammaw said. Then she hugged Catherine as though she wanted her to stay forever—to help plant the garden and pick the beans and eat them with fatback and be still another girl to sleep in Mammaw and Papaw's house as long as she wanted.

Daddy drove the girls to school in Papaw's car, with Catherine's bags in the trunk. He announced that he'd found a man who would trade him a six-year-old Chevy pickup for labor: Daddy would be putting a fence around the man's two acres of land. The deal had been closed with a handshake, and Daddy was pleased.

"Guess you come at the worst possible time," he told Catherine, "but you look at it another way, maybe it was for the best. If ever Ivy June needed company, it was now."

The rescue of the five miners was the chief topic of conversation at school. Whose cousin had been on the rescue team, whose aunt had volunteered for the Red Cross, which ma had driven an ambulance?

There was an assembly of thanksgiving in the gym first period, and two minutes of silence for the two miners who had died. Ivy June bowed her head without guilt this time, grateful beyond words that Papaw had been spared, sorrowful for the families of the miners who had been swept away.

"You'll have a lot to tell back in Lexington, won't you?" Mary Beth said to Catherine as they walked back to their classes.

"To tell it's one thing," said Catherine. "To be here— that's something else."

Together, Ivy June and Catherine gave their mostly finished report about celebrations and festivals, city and country, and it was a relief to talk—to *think*—about anything else. The class laughed when Ivy June repeated the snipe-hunting story that Papaw had told them. She was surprised when Luke Weller spoke up, a one-sided grin on his face:

"I had that trick played on me once when I went to visit my cousins," he said. "Only, I caught on to what they were fixing to do, and after they left me holding the sack, I hightailed it back to the house and got there before they did."

Everyone laughed some more, and Ivy June felt that if she had done nothing else that day but make Luke Weller grin, it was something.

At lunchtime, Ivy June was surprised that a few of the other girls brought little going-away gifts for Catherine. They didn't offer used clothes, as the girls in Lexington had offered Ivy June. Mary Beth gave Catherine a little bar of homemade soap with a real violet pressed in the top, and Angela gave her a pen with three different colors of ink.

Shirl's gift was rolled up and tied with a pink ribbon, and Catherine unfurled a huge, triple-extra-large T-shirt with the words *One Big Happy* . . . on the front. Catherine shrieked with delight, and so did the others.

"He did it!" Shirl explained. "Fred Mason's cousin ate the four-foot sub all by himself—had three witnesses—and he got the big T-shirt and gave it to me."

"It's big enough for two people!" Catherine said, holding it up.

"Well, let's see!" said Shirl, and immediately, standing back to back, the two girls pulled the enormous T-shirt over their heads, two arms sticking out each sleeve, four legs out the bottom, and tried to walk together. They even had the eighth graders laughing, Jimmy Harris included.

When school was over, Ivy June walked out to the parking lot with Miss Dixon and Catherine. Mrs. Fields would be waiting for Catherine at the library in Hazard.

"Flora's going to be at the house to help me get it ready for Mom," Catherine explained. "I want to put up a Welcome Home sign on the porch. I'm going to have lunch ready for her too, and sort of be her nurse till she's well." She suddenly flung her arms around Ivy June.

"Goodbye," she said into the side of her neck, and Ivy

June could feel her swallow. "Thank you for everything. If we wrote a story about this, no one would believe it all happened in the same week, would they?"

"Never," Ivy June agreed. "Can't hardly believe it myself." She glanced over at her teacher. "What do you always tell us? That real life is stranger than stories?"

"I believe it's 'truth is stranger than fiction,' " Miss Dixon said. "I'm glad you remembered that."

"It's strange, all right." Catherine hugged Ivy June one last time, and as she got in the car, she whispered, "Hang on to your lucky rock, Ivy June."

Ivy June grinned. "It's yours now—something to remember me by. Check your pocket."

CHAPTER THIRTY-NINE

July 4

Seems like a year since I wrote in my journal. Everything I had to share with the class, I already told straight out. Didn't read any of this. Too personal.

Papaw retired from the mine yesterday, and we didn't need any fireworks to celebrate. Daddy got us some sparklers, though, and the Hedges came down with their grandkids, and I mean we had these little lights traveling up and down the hill from Mammaw's to Ma's, all of us shrieking and carrying on. When the sparklers burned down, all that gunpowder smell filling our noses, I just sat on the porch looking up at the stars, thinking what

Papaw said once about the dark being bright compared to the mine. Thinking about how he never has to go in there again.

We're going to Cutshin tomorrow and get us a dog from the Prathers. That was something else Papaw said he was going to do when he retired. The Prathers' hound had puppies couple months ago, and Papaw says it's about time our cats got a little excitement.

Shirl came over on Memorial Day—Decoration Day, as Grandmommy still calls it—and after we'd been to the cemetery, we sat on the porch watching cars go by on the road the other side of the creek. Bet we counted twenty cars in an hour. People from Cincinnati or Cleveland or Morgantown or wherever they moved to, all coming back to visit the graves, just like they do every year.

"Last Decoration Day for somebody," Grandmommy said, and she knows it could well be her. But she also knows that if it is her that's gone, she'll be buried over there beside Grandpappy, and we'll all be there, making wreaths of summer flowers. We'll sit in the shade with the other folks we see once a year and talk about all the times Thunder Creek was flooded, who's moving away and who's coming back.

I made a wreath for Mr. Weller's grave. They never could afford a headstone, but there's a marker with his name on it. I wanted Luke to know that somebody thought to bring flowers for his daddy, same as I'd want him to do for Papaw, if it was him.

Catherine's mom is doing okay. I've had two letters from Cat since she left, and I've so far sent her one. She wants to know if we can call ourselves half sisters. Says you can say that without people asking how it got to be half. So I can call myself Ivy June Combs sometimes if I want, and she can call herself Catherine Mosley, just for the fun of it. She jokes that she'll send me a picture of her every Memorial Day if I'll send her one of me on Decoration Day.

When we're both eighteen, we're going to get together no matter where we are, and we're going to squeeze into that ONE BIG HAPPY T-shirt and let somebody take our picture.

And because truth is stranger than fiction, maybe I'll move to Lexington, she tells me. Maybe we'll both of us move to Cleveland. Or it just might be that I'll go to college and she'll be there, and we'll end up roommates. It could happen.

Ivy June Mosley

ABOUT THE AUTHOR

Phyllis Reynolds Naylor's books take place in many different states and settings, but rural areas are among her favorites. Her father was born in Mississippi, though his parents later moved to Maryland, and her mother was born in Iowa. Phyllis herself was born in Indiana, and vacations were usually spent on her paternal grandparents' farm in Maryland or on her maternal grandparents' farm in Iowa. When she received a grant from the National Endowment for the Arts, Phyllis and her husband, Rex, traveled through the little mountain communities of West Virginia and Kentucky, and coal country also captured her interest.

Mrs. Naylor is the author of 135 books, including the Newbery Award–winning *Shiloh* and the twelve books of her boy/girl battle series, which begins with *The Boys Start the War* and *The Girls Get Even*. She and her husband live in Gaithersburg, Maryland. They are the parents of two grown sons and the grandparents of Sophia, Tressa, Garrett, and Beckett.

YEARLING!

Looking for more great books to read?
Check these out!

- ❏ *All-of-a-Kind Family* by Sydney Taylor
- ❏ *Are You There God? It's Me, Margaret* by Judy Blume
- ❏ *Blubber* by Judy Blume
- ❏ *The City of Ember* by Jeanne DuPrau
- ❏ *Crash* by Jerry Spinelli
- ❏ *The Girl Who Threw Butterflies* by Mick Cochrane
- ❏ *The Gypsy Game* by Zilpha Keatley Snyder
- ❏ *Heart of a Shepherd* by Rosanne Parry
- ❏ *The King of Mulberry Street* by Donna Jo Napoli
- ❏ *The Mailbox* by Audrey Shafer

- ❏ *Me, Mop, and the Moondance Kid* by Walter Dean Myers
- ❏ *My One Hundred Adventures* by Polly Horvath
- ❏ *The Penderwicks* by Jeanne Birdsall
- ❏ *Skellig* by David Almond
- ❏ *Soft Rain* by Cornelia Cornelissen
- ❏ *Stealing Freedom* by Elisa Carbone
- ❏ *Toys Go Out* by Emily Jenkins
- ❏ *A Traitor Among the Boys* by Phyllis Reynolds Naylor
- ❏ *Two Hot Dogs with Everything* by Paul Haven
- ❏ *When My Name Was Keoko* by Linda Sue Park

Visit **www.randomhouse.com/kids** for additional reading suggestions
in fantasy, adventure, mystery, and humor!